The Invisible Cult in Choctaw County

The Invisible Cult in Choctaw County

A Pilot and Pianist Murder Mystery

MW Burdette

This is a work of fiction. Names, characters, businesses, places, events and incidents are either the products of the author's imagination or used in a fictitious manner. Any resemblance to actual persons, living or dead, or actual events is purely coincidental.

© 2022 MW Burdette. All rights reserved. Printed in the United States of America. For information, contact Amazon.com at www.amazon.com.

ISBN-13: 9798565649758

Original Publication Date: 2022. Published in the United States of America by Amazon.com.

For Martha

CONTENTS

INTRODUCTION

Prologue

PART I: Unhealthy History

    Abrupt Change in Direction
    Mystery and Suspicion
    A History of Violence
    A Clannish People
    Local Rumors
    Facts or Fiction
    Revelation
    An Ally in Butler
    Testing the Waters

PART II: Exposing the Guilty

    Narrowing the Suspects List
    The Pow Wow
    Hiding in Plain Sight
    Taking a Chance
    Some Friendly Assistance
    Unwitting Helper
    The Raid

Prologue

The Misery Index was created in the 1970's by little known economist Arthur Okun of the Brookings Institute. Basically, Okun stated that the Misery Index is the sum of the current inflation rate plus the seasonally adjusted unemployment rate at any particular time in history. For example, if the unemployment rate is 5.0% and the inflation rate is 3.5%, the Misery Index is 8.5%. The supposition is that as the Misery Index increases, murders and other crimes rise in tandem with the Misery Index. During the Carter Administration in the 1970s, the Misery Index climbed as high as 16.26, indicating that the county's financial health was in deep trouble. While the lowest Misery Index for any president since Harry Truman was Donald Trump at 6.60.

Why is that important in modern-day society? Statistics gathered over long periods of time, four years or more, indicate that when the Misery Index is high there are more issues with civil unrest, financial uncertainty in the New York Stock Exchange, and a general lack of confidence in the federal government by its citizens. The goal of every Presidential Administration should be to minimize the Misery Index while expanding the productivity of its citizens, thereby creating a feeling of self-worth among its citizenries.

Historically, Choctaw County, Alabama, had been falling behind its sister counties for years in financial stability and growth. The Misery Index for Choctaw County was off the charts! In the early 1920s, Choctaw County had been a booming area, with sawmills and lumber companies which flourished until they collapsed during the Great Depression. The first oil well in Alabama was drilled in Choctaw County in 1944, and oil and gas became the most important industry for the next thirty years, until the industry waned in the 1970s due to the wells losing profitability. Since that time, Choctaw County had slipped in per capita income to the point that over 34% of the population was living below the poverty line. Just two hours south of Choctaw County, Mobile was a booming metropolis with state docks, agricultural industries, and manufacturing concerns driving their economy. The county seat of Choctaw County, Butler, Alabama, could not brag about how it had handled the many changes that had come to the state in the last 100 years.

Choctaw County, Alabama, is not the kind of place one stumbles into by accident. The county was established on December 29, 1847, by an act of the Alabama Legislature, but the Choctaw tribe of Native Americans had existed in the area as part of the original indigenous residents prior to any Europeans settling on the North American Continent. They were unceremoniously pushed out of their homeland and relocated to a reservation in the Oklahoma Territory by an act of the U.S. Congress in the 1831, and the Choctaws were one of the largest tribes of Native American that traveled on the Trial of Tears to the Southwest U.S.A. Historians tell us that when the Spanish and French began trading with the Choctaw Indians, there were more than 15,000 local Native American residents located in Mississippi and Southwest Alabama alone. Although the Choctaw Nation, under the leadership of Chief Pushmataha, fought with the United States against the French and other European invaders to preserve the nation, the Choctaws were still required to surrender their lands to the U.S. Government. Eventually, after the Treaty of Doak's Stand, the Choctaws were required to relocate to Arkansas. By 1830, all the Choctaws were removed from the State of Alabama and located in the western reservations created for the Native American nations. The folklore was that some of the descendants of the Choctaw Indians still reside in the hills surrounding Choctaw County, and their children and grandchildren still believe that the land of their elders was illegally stolen from them by the U.S. Government.

Apart from the Choctaws, it was reported that a gypsy caravan also took up residence in Choctaw County because of its remoteness to other cities and towns in the state. Rituals had been discovered in the wooded areas surrounding Butler, confirming that occultism was alive and well in Choctaw County. While some of the residents gave credit to the Choctaw Indians for the animal sacrifices that had been found, others believed it was the work of the gypsies who still existed in the area and who could be seen in town from time to time.

Crime had become so prevalent in Butler, Alabama, that the County Commissioners of Choctaw County hired Conrad Phillips, a retired U.S.A.F. Master Sergeant, to become the sheriff, and to restore civility and law and order to the county. Phillips had been a senior enlisted non-commissioned officer in the service, as well as an original resident of Butler before he enlisted in the U.S. Military. Butch Todd had been acquainted with Conrad when they served in Afghanistan, and he was surprised that his friend had taken the job of restoring the peace in a little town in Southwest Alabama. He was even more surprised when the county commissioner of Choctaw County had contacted Butch and told him that their circuit judge, Julius Malone, had died mysteriously, and the commissioner asked Butch to help them discover what actually happened.

PART I: Unhealthy Past

Chapter 1

Abrupt Change in Direction

"Are we really going to get away from everything for an entire week?" Claire asked Butch as they were packing his pickup truck for the trip south to Gulf Shores and the emerald water and white sands of the western coast of Florida. Summer was turning into fall, and the cooler weather would make their stay in a normally hot area more pleasant. Labor Day was just next week, and this was the last big opportunity to spend time in the sun at the beach before all the activity started diminishing up and down the Emerald Coast.

"Would I lie to you?"

"Only if it was to your benefit," she laughed. "Dealing with Uncle Sam and his convoluted interpretation of justice just about broke my spirit. Charleston would have been much more enjoyable as a retreat, rather than a fact-finding mission for a violent airplane crash where innocent military personnel were sacrificed for money or power. I hope they throw the book at that general who was complicit in the crash of the C5-A and its crew."

"Since the crash was more than just a greedy grab for money and power, the U.S. Government will probably let General Leonard Lockhart relocate under the provisions of the WITSEC program, assuming the general rolls on his fellow conspirators. Plus, if the Russians were involved in any way with the crash and theft of military secrets, public exposure to those facts might create the perfect scenario for WWIII. Since the Berlin Wall was removed, the Cold War has been relegated more to innuendo than outright threats."

"It doesn't seem fair to let General Lockhart off the hook for all the death and misery he allowed to take place under his watch. That's all I'm saying."

"Yeah, but fair play has never been the number one concern for our government, dating back to the Battle of Bunker Hill or earlier. Unfortunately, we must choose the lesser of the evils we are faced with on a daily basis. By informing the Russians that we have documented facts that they were the principal cause the C5-A crashed is like holding a large bucket of water over their heads. Contrary to what the public believes about the Russians not caring what people think of them, they need to continue to have the confidence of their own people to remain in power. When one considers that we really don't know how the Russian people perceive of their leaders, and if they really hate us as much as the propaganda spouted by Pravda, the leaders of the Russian military command are not so removed from the last revolution that brought Communism into power. While Western European countries' population basks in the sunlight of almost total freedom, along with those visibly modeled by the Americas, Russia is constantly teetering on unpopularity. Don't think that they are willing to roll the dice on whether espionage on the United States might cause the common people pain, assuming we retaliate or embargo goods that could make Ivan less happy with their leaders. In other words, we take our losses and enjoy our small successes where we can get them." Claire looked at Butch with less than a happy face.

"That doesn't mean I have to like it!"

"You are correct. Most Americans will never know what happened in Charleston, and that's probably a good thing. Trust me, having fought a real enemy with rockets and gunfire, peaceable coexistence is far more desirable than starting a real war." Claire had had enough of this garbage, so she changed the subject.

"Why don't you tell me all about this romantic place you're taking me to in Gulf Shores. I would have settled for a Gulf view on the beach in a modest hotel, but I do like fussy places as well," she gushed.

"I wouldn't say it was anything too special," he taunted her. "It's just a little bed and breakfast place that sits on a grassy knoll facing the Gulf of Mexico, with a large private beach and several no trespassing signs." He smiled at her and winked. This was his usual way of teasing her when he wanted her to think of him as being romantic. Fighter pilots were not necessarily the most thoughtful men on Earth, and Butch was no exception. However, he really adored Claire Cavendish—his partner and a professional pianist. He found it difficult to believe how they had met accidentally on the streets of Ashburn, Alabama, by crashing into each other like ships on a foggy night. And while they were more different than alike, the pairing was working out quite well. Where Butch was less likely to be as soft and cuddly as Claire might have preferred in a male partner, he was very protective and would never let any harm come to her if there were any possible way of preventing it. Claire, on the other hand, appeared to be all sugar and spice and everything nice, but she did carry a pistol and she knew how to use it. No one would have thought these two different personalities could get along, much less cohabitate.

"I want to know about the B&B. Do you have pictures?"

"No, Claire. I just saw it listed in the want ads for Gulf Shore property rentals and thought we might give it a shot. If we don't like it, we can always get a room on the beach in some hotel or condominium. I understand that after next Monday the crowds will diminish and the beaches will become almost isolated until Spring Break next February. Did you ever go to Panama City Beach or Gulf Shores when you were attending Ashburn University?"

"That information is on a 'need to know' basis, and you don't need to know!" she giggled. "I may have a few secrets that you haven't yet discovered, but you'll have to ply me with wine and dancing to get me to spill my guts about my past." She shot a wicked smile at Butch, and her answer seemed to catch him off guard.

"Mysterious lady, huh? What else don't I know about you that I should know before I get too involved?"

"If becoming my business partner, live-in roommate, and steady beau isn't involved enough for you, I don't know what would be. I'll keep my little secrets for now, and you can keep yours."

"I don't have any secrets worthy of you discovering. Can you say the same?"

"I'm not saying anything. Next subject!"

They continued driving down I-65 South, passed through the capital city of Montgomery, and read the road signs indicating that Mobile was 198 miles from their current location. Since Butch was no daredevil when he drove on the freeways, it would take 3 ½ more hours for them to arrive at their destination, so Claire decided to close her eyes and doze until they got closer to the beach. Just when she was dozing off, Butch's cell phone rang. He tried to answer it quietly, but Claire was a light sleeper and she heard Butch's end of the conversation.

"Hello. This is Butch, to whom am I speaking?" Butch didn't recognize the telephone number that was being displayed on his screen. He usually let these unidentified calls go to his message center, but he had a gut feeling that he should answer this call. He was correct.

"Butch? This is SGT Connally. Are you where you can talk?"

"Sure, Elene. I'm driving south on I-65, just north of Evergreen, Alabama. Claire and I are on our way to Gulf Shores for some R&R. What's up?"

"Can you speak to Mayor Hannity?" Butch thought that it was odd for the mayor to be tracking him down, especially since the mayor had authorized both he and Claire's absence for a week to unwind and refresh their minds after the grueling trip to Charleston.

"I can speak to the mayor. Do you have him on this call?"

"I will patch him in, and we will do a conference call. That is, if I can remember how to do that without hanging up on you. Hold on for a minute." The line clicked and Butch thought that he had been disconnected, but he heard Elene's voice come back on the line. "OK, I have Mayor Hannity on the line with us now. Can everyone hear each other?" The mayor and Butch acknowledged that they could hear each other and SGT Connally as well. By this time Claire was wide awake and looking at Butch with great interest.

"I'm going to put this call on speaker since I'm driving, and I also want Claire to hear what you have to say. Is that OK with you Mayor?"

"Absolutely, because this affects her as well." Butch nodded to Claire, and she took out a small notebook to jot down any instructions that might be given by the mayor or SGT Connally. "I'm afraid I have some bad news for both of you," Hannity said. Neither Claire nor Butch had any idea of any news that could derail them from their trip to the beach, but they would listen anyway.

"Is there some emergency that we need to be aware of, or some crisis that effects Butch and me?"

"No, it's nothing like that, but I do need both of you to assist a personal friend of mine in Choctaw County, Alabama, with a serious matter. He just contacted me and told me about a crisis that they are going through in Butler, and I assured him that you and Claire would stop by on your way to Gulf Shores to see if you could assist him. I don't think it will take you long to determine if you can help, and for every hour you are detained by detouring to his town you can add it back at the end of your week at the beach. I hate to ask you to help, but Conrad Phillips and I go back a long way in police work, and I would feel obliged if you could look in on him." Butch thought that this was more of a request than an order, but the request was coming from the man who controlled both his and Claire's future employment, so there really was no decision to make.

"We will be glad to look in on your old friend, Mayor. I haven't been to Butler before, but according to my GPS it is about forty miles to the northwest of Evergreen. I think if we take U.S. Highway 84, we can be there in about an hour or so. Will you call Sheriff Phillips and let him know that we are one our way? We have reservations at a bed and breakfast inn in Gulf Shores this evening, and if we are going to be delayed, we will need someone at the station to call them and let them know that we are running behind schedule, but we still plan to check into the inn this evening."

"I can call them for you, Butch," SGT Connally said. I'll explain that there has been an emergency, so they won't charge you for tonight's lodging in case you are delayed in Butler." Butch immediately suspected that SGT Connally and Mayor Hannity were not telling them everything about this detour, but he wouldn't confront the issue until he knew more about the mission.

"Thanks, Elene. We will call you and give you a status report after we speak to Sheriff Phillips." Butch hung up and looked at Claire. It was obvious by the angry expression on her pretty face that she didn't like this detour at all. However, she sat quietly as Butch began looking for the exit off I-65 for U.S. Highway 84 West. He hoped that their visit to Butler would be quick and decisive, and that they would be back on track to arrive in Gulf Shores by dark.

The trip from Evergreen to Butler took longer than expected, because once they arrived in southern Choctaw County the highways became less than ideal heading north to Butler, the county seat. The roads were paved, but that's about all one could say about the two-lane, asphalt ribbons of material passing for a county-maintained highway. Butch had driven dirt roads in better shape than these roads in Choctaw County. Alabama had a reputation for some of the worst schools, health care facilities, and deteriorating highways. Choctaw County was statistically one of the poorest counties in the state of Alabama, coming in 53rd out of 67, with a per capita income of only $17,214, a median household income of $31,076, compared to Shelby County's per capita income of $68,380 and a household income of over $81,000. Needless to say, the roads, schools, and public facilities in the wealthier counties were more in line with the national average than in these poorer, isolated rural counties.

There were only three officially recognized Native American casinos in the state of Alabama, and Choctaw County was not one of their locations. The Choctaw tribe had established their casino in Philadelphia, Mississippi, just 78 miles to the northwest of Butler, so even the indigenous people of Choctaw County couldn't cash in on their heritage, much like their cousins had done in Montgomery and Aliceville.

The statistics didn't lie when it came to higher education and more financially successful families, with Shelby County leading the state in those families with 42% or more family members having received a minimum of a bachelor's degree, contrasted to less than 12% of those in Choctaw County, making it rank 62 out of 67 total counties. The other fact that could not be overlooked was that it was nationally recognized that less formally educated people tended to be more superstitious than those who had had the opportunity to get more education. Added to the natural phenomenon of the fear of the unknown, Choctaw County had other factors with which many of its surrounding county neighbors didn't have to contend. The Choctaw Indians had been rounded up by decree for the march of the Trail of Tears from their native lands in Mississippi and Alabama to Oklahoma. The Treaty of Dancing Rabbit Creek in 1831 set things in motion for the eventual demise and dismantling of the proud Choctaw Nation. Those who either couldn't or wouldn't join the march disappeared into the thick wooded areas surrounding Butler, Alabama, as well as many other cities and towns in Mississippi. At one time the state of Mississippi was principally occupied by the Choctaw Nation, and in the early 19th Century the Choctaw Indian Nation was the third largest Native American tribe in the United States. Besides the death of many Native Americans on their journey to the reservations in Oklahoma, they were hunted down and murdered by local clans and those who wished to purge the state of Alabama from them. Over the years rumors of visions of shadowy Native Americans could be seen walking through the wooded areas of Choctaw County, seeking revenge for the harm done to them and their families. Any time a person or animal disappeared without a logical explanation from Butler or its surrounding area the angry spirits of the Choctaw Indians were suspected and blamed. While angry blacks were fighting for recognition of their equal rights under the law, the Native Americans in the United States were shunned or outright displaced without cause. The very race of people who had been the indigenous people of North America were being wiped out and no one seemed to care. But as Butch and Claire got more distant from the populated areas of the state of Alabama, they began to feel an ominous pressure to assist Sheriff Phillips in any way they could to help him keep the peace in this remote area of the previous center of the Choctaw Nation in the state of Alabama. Butch couldn't explain the feeling, and he really didn't have all the facts at that point, but there was something or someone pleading for his and Claire's help. They finally pulled into Butler, stopped in front of the Choctaw County Courthouse, and got out of their vehicles. Butler was so small, less than 2500 people residing within the city limits, that a strange vehicle with two unknown people had the majority of the observers looking around like a bobble-head doll trying to get a good peek at the visitors.

"Do you feel like a specimen under a microscope?" asked Claire? Butch had observed the stares as well as the finger-pointing from those sitting outside the small cafes that surrounded the county courthouse. It was a typical country town scene—farmers in bib overalls, women in simple flowered cotton dresses, and kids with dirty faces and dirty cloths. If Butch tried a little, he could imagine this scene was one from a movie about the Great Depression.

"I've seen a lot of sad looking people from all over the world, but none of them sadder looking than the faces in Butler," he said. "Let's see if we can find Sheriff Phillips, get our task done, and be on our way to Gulf Shores." They walked into the historic old courthouse and marveled at its appearance.

According to recorded history, Choctaw County was founded in December of 1847 and was named for the Choctaw Tribe of Native Americans who were the indigenous people in the area. Most of the early European American pioneers of Choctaw County were farmers from North and South Carolina, and the county's population peeked in the late 1930s and early 1940s due to the local papermill and short line railroad which were both later closed due to the arrival of the Great Depression. While the apparel industry, as well as discoveries of oil and gas, helped the county continue to exist, damage to many structures and businesses from Hurricane Frederic in 1979 eventually was the death knell for both the railroad and the apparel industries. The current Choctaw County Courthouse was built in 1906 and was the replacement building for the original structure that burned in 1871. There had been few changes in the old yellow brick façade of the building since its original construction. Still, it was odd to see this magnificent example of architecture in such a small, poor city in the middle of nowhere. As they entered the building they observed a lofty ceiling with hand carved moldings, ornate matching staircases on each end of the large main floor, and solid wooden antique doors to each and every office on the first floor. The doors appeared to be over eight feet in height, four feet in width, and constructed of some type of solid hardwood. Multiple slowly rotating fans hung from the ceiling which helped to cool the massive lobby area of the old building. Butch estimated the ceiling to be at least thirty feet high, giving the courthouse an overall feeling of expanse. Fortunately, there was an information desk available, and Butch and Claire approached the senior volunteer for directions to Sheriff Phillips' office. The little woman sitting behind the massive oak desk appeared to be in her eighties, but she had a sparkle in her eyes that made Claire smile.

"Pardon me, but can you tell us where Sheriff Phillips' office is located?" Claire asked. The nameplate on the desk revealed that the hostess' name was

Tallulah Ashalintubbi, and Claire had to ask its meaning. "By the way, do you pronounce your name *Ta-loo-la*?"

"Yes, I do. And my last name is pronounced A*sh-a-lin-too-be*. My first name means 'Leaping Water.' I am 100% Choctaw Indian," she said proudly, and my great-great-great grandfather was on the trail of tears back in the 19th century. It is remembered as the saddest day in the history of our Choctaw Nation." Claire thought she detected a tear in Tallulah's bright blue eyes, so she moved on to the reason for their visit.

"We have an appointment to see Sheriff Phillips. Can you tell us which office is his, and do you need to call ahead for us?"

"Oh, no, Honey. We aren't so formal here in Butler. You don't need an appointment or to be announced to the Sheriff. His office is on the second floor, the third door from the top of the staircase on the left. He is usually in his office, unless he tells me otherwise, and he has not done so this morning." Claire and Butch thanked Tallulah and began the long climb to the top of the staircase.

"We should have asked her if they had an elevator," Butch complained.

"It wouldn't hurt us to get a little exercise, Butch. And it wouldn't surprise me if this place didn't have an elevator anyway. There doesn't look like any improvements have been made since it was built 100 years ago."

"Oh, I'm sure there's an elevator. Every municipal building is mandated to have access for the physically handicapped. I'll ask the sheriff just to satisfy my curiosity."

"Would you like to make a bet on whether or not they have a lift?" Claire asked. Butch's competitive spirit came alive, and he agreed to bet her breakfast in bed on the outcome of the question. He hated taking advantage of Claire, but everyone knew that mandates on safety and personal access from the federal government was almost always complied with by city and county administrations as well.

"We'll ask the sheriff when we see him. If anyone can give us the facts on such things it will be the sheriff." Claire agreed and they finally finished climbing the long curving staircase, turned left at the landing as instructed by Tallulah, and started down the hall toward the door marked Choctaw County Sheriff's Department. They pushed the heavy door open and walked up to the counter which separated the employees from the visitors. Presenting his business card, Butch asked to speak to the sheriff. In less than a minute they saw a short, stout man in a tan uniform approaching them.

"You must be Sam's detectives," the sheriff said.

"I'm Butch Todd, the Ashburn Police Chief, and this is Claire Cavendish, my Chief of Detectives. Mayor Hannity said you were having some issues and he thought we might be of assistance to you."

"Please come in and take a seat," Sheriff Phillips said as he motioned to his office and the two padded chairs facing his desk. Phillips went behind the desk, took his chair, and asked them if they would like coffee or tea to drink as they visited.

"We're fine, Sheriff," Butch said. "Can you tell us how we might help you?"

"I'm afraid it may not be that easy to educate you on our issues, but I will do my best," the sheriff said, which prompted Butch to glance at Claire and they exchanged looks of concern. This was shaping up to be more than they had bargained for. "Are either of you believers in the occult or other religious traditions?" Claire was the first to answer, and she approached the sheriff's question analytically.

"When you use term occult, I am assuming you're using the general definition of the occult as being a category of supernatural beliefs and practices which generally fall outside the scope of religion and science. Would it be safe to assume that's what you mean?"

"Yes and no," Conrad Phillips said with a big sigh.

"Yes, and no?" Butch repeated the sheriff's rather ambiguous answer to Claire's question. "Can you elaborate a little on how both answers are applicable in your case? We want to help if we can, but we need to be on the same page as far as the basis we are considering."

"How much do you two know about the Choctaw Native American tribe?"

"Not that much," Claire said. "I know they were one of the larger tribes in the Southern United States before they were forced to walk to Oklahoma and relocate to the reservations established for them by the U.S. Government. I'm not sure how many more facts than that Butch is aware, but that pretty much exhausts my knowledge of a proud people." Butch chose to not answer the sheriff's question, thereby establishing that he had nothing to add to Claire's response. A big smile appeared on Conrad's face, and his next comment was a revelation to both Claire and Butch.

"It's almost lunchtime, so why don't you two let me treat you to a nice county cooked meal at the local café across the street. It may take me a few minutes to explain the depth of my real concerns, as they are steeped in the history of the Choctaw Indian Nation." He motioned them toward the door, and they followed him without resistance.

"By the way," Claire asked, "does this building have an elevator?"

"No, we don't. I know we're not in compliance with the federal mandates of all public buildings to have an escalator or elevator for handicapped patrons, but this courthouse was built almost 100 years ago, and it falls under the 'grandfathered clause' in the law. We looked into installing an elevator, but once it became political in nature to either install or not install an elevator, the idea was abandoned."

"Political in nature?" Claire asked. "I don't understand." The sheriff laughed to himself before answering Claire's question.

"You're from a small town, aren't you?" He directed his conversation to both Claire and Butch.

"We are," Butch answered for both of them.

"Do you have small-town politics in Ashburn?"

"I guess we do," Clair answered. "What has that to do with an elevator in the courthouse?"

"Well, you haven't been here very long, so I will explain it to you as best I can. Choctaw County is the previous home of the Choctaw Nations, along with a large portion of East Mississippi. When it was finally established that Butler was to be the county seat, they decided to build a courthouse, and decided to bring Choctaw County into the twentieth century, there was a lot of pushbacks from the locals. You must remember that Choctaw County is unique in the state of Alabama in that it was once Native American owned and populated. Only after treaties with the natives, some underhanded politics to encourage them to move as a tribe to the Oklahoma Territory and gerrymandering of voting precincts did Choctaw County began its history of being managed by the white man. Many local natives moved into the hills and surrounding forests to avoid moving to Oklahoma. Supposedly, they are still thriving in the rural and unchartered areas of the county, but no one knows how many are left and where their locations are. Anyway, when we decided to add an elevator to the courthouse a local politician who wanted to be sheriff started a campaign stating that my health was so bad that we had to have an elevator to get to our office, so that idea was quelched."

"And you don't have to install one in accordance with federal law and building guidelines?" Claire asked.

"Nope. Buildings older than 50 years were grandfathered to be historical in nature and not required to change things like adding elevators, air-conditioning, and other *modern* features. Since most courthouses have been remodeled since the 1950s and 1960s, most have had to comply once they filed for a permit to change the structure. We added air-conditioning and central heat back in the 1970s, but nothing new has been added since then. Also, you must remember that we are one of the poorest counties in the state of Alabama, and that's saying something!"

"In that case, Sheriff, we'll take the stairs!" Butch said.

Chapter 2

Mystery and Suspicion

The walk to Alice's Restaurant was less than 200 feet from the front door of the courthouse, and they were seated and ordering their drinks in less than five minutes. The waitress was named Donna, and she brought Sheriff Phillips a tall glass of sweet, iced tea without him having to order it. She took a small green order pad from her apron and asked Butch and Claire what they wanted to drink.

"I'll have unsweet iced tea," Claire said. The waitress frowned and shook her head.

"Hun, we don't have unsweet iced tea. I can get you a diet cola or a glass of water, but we sweeten all the tea before we open up in the morning." Butch stifled a laugh, ordered water and black coffee, and waited for Claire to respond to Donna.

"Just water," Claire said. "That will be fine."

"What will y'all have for lunch?" She looked specifically at the sheriff who indicated a "number 2" by holding up two fingers. Claire and Butch looked at the menu board above the counter and saw that a "number 1" was fried chicken; a "number 2" was meatloaf and gravy; and a "number 3" was vegetable soup with homemade cornbread. Claire ordered a number 3, and Butch ordered a number 2.

"We like things simple here in Choctaw County," Conrad Phillips said. "Donna could have brought me the meatloaf and gravy without my ordering it, but she was being polite." Claire and Butch just nodded to the sheriff and Conrad began to speak. Claire gave Butch one of those "uh huh" looks, and they proceeded with their questions.

"Sheriff, our boss said that you had some concerns which you wanted to discuss with us. What were they?" Butch asked. Conrad looked over each shoulder for possible spies before he spoke.

"We think we may have a cult operating in our area, and I'm not sure how to determine the seriousness of that discovery."

"What do you mean by cult?" Claire asked.

"As I may have indicated before, Choctaw County is unlike any other county in the state of Alabama. Besides being the original home of the Choctaw Native American tribe, the Civil War was fought with ferocity in these parts. It's possible that the renegade Choctaw Indians have teamed up with the KKK to form an unlikely alliance to prevent us from governing the area like a civilized people." For some reason this statement made no sense at all to Claire and Butch. Conrad could see that they were fighting to discern exactly what he meant, so he elaborated. "I know what you're thinking. How does the remnant of the Choctaw Nation and the KKK have anything in common?"

"That did cross my mind," Butch admitted with a grin.

"The Choctaw Nations was exactly that—a nation. While generally a peace-loving group of people, when they were forced to go to war they did as all conquering nations did. They added territory to their currently owned property, and all survivors of the battles became subjects— slaves, if you will—of the Choctaw Nation. They were looked upon as property, much like the Africans had been viewed by the plantation owners of the South during the

Civil War. The only difference in the two approaches to slavery was that one people purchased the slaves from slave traders, and the other people bested their captives on the field of battle. The main difference in the two nations was that it was not considered a curse or a blemish on one's character to fail in battle, assuming one fought with honor and dignity. The survivors of the Native American battles were folded into the conquering tribe and assimilated into the greater community. While they never became part of the Choctaw tribe, they did hold status as productive members of the community. However, if you look at the African slaves brought to America and sold on the open market as property, you will see that they were never assimilated into the Southern culture, other than being property owned by the plantation barons, and those who profited by their manual labor. Even the house slaves were never considered family, even after several generations were born into the family of the slave owners."

"I understand the likenesses and differences in the conquered people by the Choctaws and the African slaves brought to America to be slaves forever. How does that factor into your situation in Choctaw County?" Butch asked.

"That's the amazing thing about these two peoples. They shared the experience of ownership of an underclass of people, and they shared the fact that the U.S. Government took their possessions away from them in the relocation of the Choctaw Indians to Oklahoma on the Trail of Tears, and the loss of the slaves to the South in the Civil War. That seems to be what has bonded these two unlike groups of people together."

"How many descendants of the Choctaw Nation do you think are hiding in the hills of Southwest Alabama?" Claire asked. "It couldn't be too many, or they would be discovered over time. After all, wasn't the Trail of Tears march back in the early 20th century?"

"Actually, the purge of the five major Native American tribes began in 1831, well before the Civil War began. It was over by the early 1850s, years before the Civil War broke out between the Confederates and the Union Army."

"You're telling us that you think the two dissatisfied parties have teamed up to cause issues in your area over 150 years after both were wronged by the U.S. Government?" Claire asked. "Do you have any physical proof to support your theory?" The sheriff nodded and opened a pocket on his uniform, retrieved a folded note, and spread it out before Claire and Butch.

"Read this note and then you tell me if I'm imagining this whole thing."

Butch and Claire read the note and looked up simultaneously into the eyes of a wise, seasoned county sheriff. They had a difficult time believing what they were reading. The note read, "It's time to unite in our cause to regain what rightfully belongs to each of our peoples. Rise up!" The signatures on the note were from the Grand Dragon of the KKK in Choctaw County, as well as the Chief in Exile of the Choctaw Nation, Laughing Bear.

"I read the note and I still have a difficult time believing that either of these co-signers has the authority or power to cause that much mischief," Butch said. "Since you don't know how many Choctaw Indians are involved, how do you know their presence and a remnant of the KKK can actually do that much harm in Choctaw County? Maybe it's just a warning to keep you and your department from infringing on their hiding places."

"I considered that as well. At first, I thought it was either a hoax or just a few disgruntled folks that wanted to have their case aired in a public forum. Then I got this note. Shortly thereafter, Julius Malone, our circuit judge, was mysteriously murdered in his home." Phillips pulled out a similar note to the first one and unfolded it for Butch and Claire to read. It read, "We're coming for your scalp, Carpetbagger!"

"What does that mean?" Claire asked.

"Beats me," the sheriff said. "But it scared us enough to call your boss. I had heard about the case you had solved for the U.S. Government, and I was hoping you had some clout with the people in D.C."

"It wasn't that kind of case," Butch said.

"What kind of case? A case is a case, isn't it?" Sheriff Phillips asked. Butch looked at Claire and rolled his eyes. "Uh oh. I think I may have erred in my assumption that the case you solved was open and shut. From the reaction that you gave your partner, may I assume it was a sensitive one?"

"Classified as 'Eyes Only' sensitive, Sheriff. We really can't talk about it. The U.S. Marshal Service is also involved in the resolution of that case. However, we may have a few favors owed us by a person or two at the Pentagon. I can't promise anything up front, but we will definitely listen to what you have to say and take it from there. Is that sufficient enough for you to clue us in on what's happening in Choctaw County?"

"Absolutely. Sam Hannity speaks very highly of both of you, and that's good enough for me. Maybe I should start from the beginning." Donna brought their dinners to them, balanced on her outstretched arms like a circus performer.

"Why don't we eat first, then I'd rather discuss this in your private office. There may be too many ears around here for either of us." They all three looked up from their plates and everyone in Alice's Restaurant was looking intently at them.

"Good idea, Butch." They ate their meals, made small talk about local police issues, and Butch picked up the check for their lunch.

"All that food was only $18.57?" Butch asked when Donna brought the bill.

"Yep," Conrad said. "You must remember that we are a small, poor town." He laughed at his comment, and Butch left a $20.00 tip for Donna. She seemed quite pleased as they left the restaurant. They were back across the street and in Conrad's office in a matter of minutes.

"Do you think your office is secure enough to discuss issues of national security?" Claire asked.

"National security? How does a possible cult issue become a matter of national security?" Conrad asked.

"The KKK has been a national security issue since its inception. Add to that you are talking about possible collusion with a remnant of the Choctaw Nation. That generally adds up to more than a local problem. What may happen is that the F.B.I. will want to get involved, as well as the N.S.A. and Homeland Security." Butch said.

"Really?" the sheriff asked. "I thought the F.B.I. had to be invited into an investigation by the local authorities in most cases. If I don't invite them, how can they just join in the investigation?"

"National security trumps every other issue or regulation. If the N.S.A. or Homeland decides that there is a possible danger for the U.S. Government to be at risk, all bets are off."

"Do you have to report things you discover here to them?"

"Not necessarily," Claire said. "As members of a certified police department in the United States, we are obligated to report anything to the federal authorities if it appears that national security may be compromised by any information we gather."

"Just what does that mean? Is it a judgment call on your part?"

"Yes and no, Sheriff. If we determine that a conspiracy is under way, we must report it to the N.S.A. or the F.B.I. We have no choice. Do you still want us involved in your case in Choctaw County?" He thought for a minute and Sheriff Phillips nodded yes.

"I'm afraid we're sitting on a powder keg here in Southwest Alabama, and if the feds have to get involved, then I guess that's OK. I'd prefer to keep things local, if possible."

"I don't know a local police chief or sheriff who doesn't prefer the same outcome, Sheriff, and we will keep that in mind. However, if we need to proceed with notification to a higher government authority, you'll be the first to know," Butch said.

"Fair enough," Conrad said. "Where do I start?"

"The beginning is always the best place to start," Claire said. She smiled at the sheriff, and he nodded in agreement.

Chapter 3

A History of Violence

Every city, town, unincorporated area, and remote part of the United States has stories of violence that has happened in the past. Many times, those incidents frame the reforms that take place in those areas where people populate and try to build their future lives. Some of the stories grow in importance as time goes by, some are merely a footprint in the history of an area, and some fade away over time, never to be a factor in the future. Choctaw County had its documented history of violence dating back hundreds of years. The less informed, unassuming casual observer driving through the quiet county today had no idea of the carnage and hostility that had marked the early days of the area's history. While having the general knowledge of the violence was available to the common man, understanding why some of the barbaric measures were undertaken was quite another thing.

Choctaw Indians, like their cousins the Cherokee, Creeks, Iroquois, all took scalps from their conquered enemies. These scalps were usually removed from dead Native Americans, or in some cases local settlers, and worn on a chain around the neck of the warrior. There have been reported cases of people being scalped while still alive, and some victims survived the scalp-taking, but it was common to take the scalps of the conquered enemy after they had been killed. Women and children were also scalped, showing the ability of the warrior to penetrate inside the secure areas of his enemy's strongholds. Some cases of scalping have been documented to have occurred in children no older than two months. While barbaric in nature, the conquering tribe believed that by taking the scalp of their enemy, they gained the power the enemy possessed before death. Sheriff Phillips shed more light on the situation once they were sitting in his office on the second floor of the courthouse building.

"Let's talk more about the second note you showed us. Do you think it came from a member of the shadow KKK organization operating in your county, or is it possible it may have come from a disgruntled descendant of the Choctaw Nation?" Claire asked.

"That's the thing," the sheriff said, "we just don't know. If you look at the proposed threat, language from both the Civil War and the Native American Trail of Tears period of time can be assumed to be factors. Why would one use carpetbaggers and scalping someone in the same sentence? They are two distinctive different actions based upon separate times in history."

"Yes, and no," Butch said. "If the descendants of the Choctaw Indians and the descendants of the Civil War both felt betrayed by the U.S. Government, then the statement makes a lot of sense."

"Butch, you're assuming that both parties believe that they are still at war with the U.S. Government, and the sheriff and his posse are just the easiest target of that government?" Claire asked.

"How else would you interpret such a note?" Butch asked. Claire thought for a moment and concurred that Butch was probably correct in his assumption. That recognition led to her next question to the sheriff.

"Is there anything else you haven't shared with us?" Claire sometimes thought she had a "second sense," or was somewhat clairvoyant when it came to solving mysteries. She couldn't put her finger on why she felt that way, and she couldn't press an investigation on a whim, but she was correct more than she was incorrect when following such a feeling. She thought the sheriff might be holding something back that was too horrible to discuss in genteel company.

"Why do you ask?" the sheriff immediately bristled at being suspected of withholding evidence that should have been revealed.

"Don't get upset, Sheriff," Butch said. "Claire is somewhat direct when she believes that she doesn't have all the facts in a case." Butch looked at Claire for discernment, but Claire didn't relent.

"Sheriff Phillips, Butch and I are on our way to a nice, restful vacation at Gulf Shores. If you are not going to be totally honest with us, we will have to move on and wish you the best with your problems here in Choctaw County." Claire began to stand up, gather her things, and point herself at the door.

"Please sit down," Conrad told her in a much smaller voice than he had been using before. It was almost as if he were whispering a secret to them. Defiant as before, Claire sat on the edge of the chair and gave the sheriff one more chance to fully enlighten them as to his concerns for Choctaw County. Something was missing in his previous comments, and he would either tell them now, or they would walk out the door. The door to his office had been left open when they had returned from lunch, so Conrad walked over to the door and shut it quietly. He came back around in front of them and leaned on the front of his enormous oak desk and began a story.

"I wasn't going to show you this," he said, as he opened a drawer on the side of his desk. He lifted out a sealed clear plastic envelope, placed it on the top of his desk, and asked them to look at it.

"What is it?" Claire asked. It looked like a toupee that had been run through a washing machine and dryer. It wasn't a full head of hair, but it was hair of some kind. It looked like human hair, but there was something odd about its appearance.

"As best we can determine from our coroner and her lab research, this appears to be the scalp of a human being. We can't determine how old it is, how old the victim was, or really anything else about it, other than it appears to be human. This scalp was presented to my office with the second note I showed you earlier. If I am being totally honest, that's why I called Mayor Hannity and asked for your assistance. I really don't know what we should be doing to find and neutralize whatever danger this incident poses to our county residents."

"I have read about scalping enemies by the early Native American tribes after a battle had been won, but I had no idea such a thing still occurred in this day and age," Butch said. "Are you certain that this is an authentic scalp and not just a prank?"

"Let me tell you what really concerns me. These notes do not make any demands. They simply state what is going to happen to the current community in Choctaw County, and we know for certain that the scalp is authentic. The forensics came back on the scalp, and it had been lifted from the victim within a few days of our receiving it at the sheriff's office. One can be scalped and not be murdered, but it is not a common thing for an enemy to scalp their victim and leave them alive. We haven't discovered a body that has been scalped recently, but if we find such a body you will be some of the first people to know."

35

"No demands from anyone?" Claire asked.

"None. The only implication I can concur is that this unusual cult may try to take over Choctaw County and reestablish themselves as if nothing in history has happened to the Native American or Johnny Reb! I know it's bizarre, but I really am at my wits end with this case." It was obvious to Claire and Butch that the sheriff was exhausted and needed help from someone. Whether or not that help should come from them, or the federal authorities was another question entirely.

"Have you contacted anyone at the federal level of government about the incidents that have been going on in Choctaw County recently? I would think that the F.B.I. might have an interest in preventing a threatening situation like this one from getting out of hand," Butch said.

"We really don't have any *facts* to share with anyone. No blood, no bodies, and nothing but empty threats written on scraps of notebook paper. I don't want to embarrass myself and my department by presenting such a flimsy case of potential danger to the community without more physical evidence that a crime has been committed, or may be committed, here in Choctaw County. If you don't think you can help, I will understand. I want to thank you for listening to my story, and now you can be on your way." Butch was staring out of the window of the sheriff's office, and it appeared that he was thinking about all the things Conrad had shared with them.

"Will you give us a moment to talk in private? I want to share some of my thoughts with Claire and get her to do the same with me." Butch looked at the clock on the wall and saw that it was 2:00 PM. Why don't we meet here again at 3:00 PM, and we will have some kind of recommendation for you?"

"That's fine. I don't know how much you can actually help, but just listening to my story helps my mental stability. At times, I think I'm going crazy!" He chuckled, but Butch knew it was no laughing matter. Butch and Claire left Sheriff Phillips' office, walked a few hundred feet from the courthouse door, and sat on an uncomfortable concrete bench that had been placed on the grounds of the Choctaw County Courthouse more than 100 years ago. There were carvings noting some of the heroes of the Civil War, Southerners of course, and the bench had been painted so many times they could not decide exactly what color the bench was initially when it was installed. Claire was the first to speak.

"What do we do, Chief?" she asked. "After all, you are my superior, and I take my lead from you." Butch laughed, knowing that she was making the statement "tongue in cheek," so to say. He always consulted with Claire on major decisions because she was very smart, and her basic instincts were rarely wrong.

"The first thing we do is determine what *we* want to do. Then we call Mayor Hannity and see if he will let us postpone our vacation. I think the sheriff has a real problem; maybe more dangerous than even he recognizes. If you and I decide to help him, we will call the mayor and see if he will let us use this time as regular worktime. As much as I want to help Conrad Phillips, I don't want to lose the off time with you at the beach in your bikini!"

"You're horrible!" she said. "What makes you think that I even put in a bikini for the beach trip?"

"What beautiful woman goes to the public beach without a bikini? My only question is: 'How big is your bikini?'"

"Wouldn't you like know?" she teased.

"Seriously, do you think we should get involved in something as crazy as a potential Native American and KKK cult, if that is the case here?"

"The man is in over his head, Butch. He seems like a nice enough fellow, but he was probably elected on a ballot without any real thought as to how he might interrupt a cult's operation in Choctaw County. If he had to do it all over, he might not even want the job."

"Is that a vote in favor of helping him?"

"I guess it is. How can we leave him in such a mess? He needs us!"

"That's true. Now, we just need to ask our esteemed boss what he thinks about us helping his friend solve his dilemma." Butch took his cell phone out of his pocket and dialed Ashburn City Hall. He asked for Mayor Hannity, waited for the familiar "What's up" from his boss, and began explaining Sheriff Phillips' need for their services. After a brief explanation, Hannity asked the magic question.

"Do you believe that Sheriff Phillips has a legitimate reason for concern?"

"Yeah, but I'm not sure that we are the ones to help him with his dilemma. I would think that the federal agencies might be more effective, and they surely have many more assets in their arsenal of weapons to use against such a cult, assuming one really does exist."

"Knowing what you know now, as far as facts are available for proof of this cult, would you call in the N.S.A. or the F.B.I.? Put yourself in Conrad's shoes and then make the judgment call." The mayor said nothing else while Butch pondered how he could honestly answer his boss' question.

"I think the F.B.I. would laugh at him and place him in that special group of fanatics that they keep an active file on. The N.S.A. would be even worse, because how does a local cult issue become a matter of national security? If bombs or explosives were detected, the ATF would be the agency to contact, not necessarily Homeland Security. I think our friend is stuck until something more definitive and horrible occurs. By that time, it may be too late to prevent widespread violence, injury, and death." Claire thought it might be good to have a counterargument to Butch's assumption of an invisible cult or empire operating in Choctaw County.

"There is the possibility that this could be a hoax or some kind, some elaborate joke being placed on the old sheriff in an election year designed to help derail his reelection campaign," Claire said. "We don't have evidence that this is *not* a genuine issue, but I think we should consider both possibilities before we commit to any action moving forward." Mayor Hannity remained silent on the other end of the telephone so long that Butch had to ask if he were still on the call.

"I'm here, and I want you two detectives to decide if we need to help the sheriff. If you chose to help him, I will get some help from Cullman County to cover for you two while you are out of the city. I will also see that your vacation time is restored 100% so you can resume your vacation as soon as you help the sheriff determine how to confront his impending crisis. However, I'm not going to tell you to help him just because he is a personal friend, and I don't want for this to go down as a personal favor or something that is not completely authorized by our office and the Ashburn Police Department. We have helped other agencies before, and, assuming what Conrad has told you is true, the mission appears to be an honorable one. So, you choose." The mayor once again became mute, and it was obvious to Butch and Claire that they had to decide the fate of their newest friend. Butch looked at Claire, got nothing from her return glance, and made the decision that helping Sheriff Phillips was a good, sound one. For better or worse, they would jump into the fray, and let the chips fall where they might.

"We're going to let the sheriff know that we will be at his disposal for the next few days, and we will do our best to investigate what is actually happening in Choctaw County related to any cult or other organization possibly operating outside the boundaries of the law."

"How long do you think it will take you to get to the bottom of things there?" Hannity asked.

"To tell you the truth, Mayor, I have no idea. If we haven't turned up something significant in a few days, we will rethink our decision to help. Does that sound fair to you?"

"More than fair, Butch. Anything you can do to help my old friend will be most appreciated." The mayor hung up and Claire began to smile.

"What?" demanded Butch. "Would you have done anything differently if you had been in charge?"

"No," she said. "But if anyone asks, I'm going to tell them that you are a big softie!"

Butch and Claire headed back into the courthouse and took the stairs up to Sheriff Phillips' office. He looked up when they knocked, and he invited them into the office once more.

"Well, what did you decide? Can you help us or not?"

"We will see what we can do, Sheriff. However, for us to continue beyond a few days we will need to uncover something significant or else we will have to move on."

"Fair enough," he said, putting out his hand to the detectives to shake on their agreement of cooperation. "I believe you'll find plenty of things that will concern you, but I'll leave that up to you." Butch and Claire shook the sheriff's hand warmly, turned to leave his office, and he gave them a parting message. "All I ask is that you keep an open mind." They exited the courthouse and began looking for a suitable place to spend the night in Butler.

Chapter 4

A *Clannish People*

It was not to be unexpected that Butler, Alabama, population of 2419 people, would be a clannish sort of town. People didn't readily talk to strangers, that is, anyone they hadn't known most of their lives, about issues the town, county, or the state might be experiencing. It wasn't anyone's business but local folks, was their attitude most of the time, but Butch and Claire also came from a small-town setting so they knew how to approach these people who might hold the keys to the knowledge that they needed to help determine if there was an illegal cult operating in Choctaw County. They needed to make friends with a local who wasn't afraid to speak to strangers. Most of the time, these strangers fell into two groups: kids and the elderly. Kids were not nearly as suspicious of people outside of their own culture, and the elderly would talk a streak to anyone willing to listen.

"I want to speak to the sheriff again, Claire."

"We just left his office an hour ago. What can he possibly tell us now that he did not tell us then?"

"Butch, we both know that the average person on the street in Butler, Alabama, will not talk honestly to us about anything happening in their town. They may be indirect descendants of the Choctaw Nation, or they may have African American blood in their backgrounds. You and I come from small towns, we work for a police department in a small town, and we know how small-town folks think and react to people whom they are not familiar with. Right?"

"They don't trust them," Butch agreed.

"Correct. And I have a foolproof way to get some local information without stirring up the water too much."

"I'm listening."

"We need to get Sheriff Phillips to introduce us to some people at the nursing home, as well as the children under the age of eighteen while they are in school. He is the ultimate authority figure in Choctaw County, and he has the confidence of the older people who reside in the adult housing facilities."

"You mean nursing homes?"

"Nursing homes, public housing, the general hospital, and all places where people who have lived long enough to overcome their inbred fear of strangers gather."

"Why are you so sure he will have a positive effect upon the local folks? Some of them might dislike and distrust him."

"Let me draw a parallel for you. I am sure that there are people in Ashburn who are jealous of you and me, but that's just human nature. That doesn't mean that more of them don't respect us and our positions of authority than those who do. After all, we don't need everyone in Butler to like or trust us—just enough to give us a good idea of whether or not there is a cult operating in Choctaw County." Claire thought for a moment, nodded her head in agreement, and began to get out of Butch's truck.

"Which group of people should we approach first?"

"Let's talk to the sheriff and get his ideas. If we can convince him that the overall idea is his, we may have more success." They went back into the courthouse and asked to see Sheriff Phillips. In a matter of minutes, they were standing in front of the sheriff, and he had a confused expression on his face.

"Did I miss something?" Phillips said with a grin. "I could swear that you two were here just an hour ago."

"No, you didn't miss anything, Sheriff," Claire said. "Butch and I were discussing how to get some of the local folk to open up to us, and we thought an introduction from you might do the trick."

"I'm listening."

"Butch and I believe that if you introduce us at the local Rotary Club, retirement homes, and public-school forums that the local people will be more inclined to open up to us. Otherwise, we are just outsiders with whom they should be suspicious of." Sheriff Phillips thought for a moment and nodded his head.

"OK. I can do that. Where do we start?" Butch and Claire told the sheriff that they were going to formulate a plan and let him know where they would be needing his involvement. He agreed, and they promptly left his office again.

"That went well!" Claire said. "I'm surprised he rolled over so easily."

"He has agreed to be involved. We don't know how he will react if he is put under political pressure to not cooperate with us somewhere down the line."

"You're just a skeptic," Claire said, giving Butch a pat on the back. "You must believe!" she said and laughed.

"I'm from Missouri," Butch fired back at Claire. "I'll believe it when I see it."

"You have to have more faith in people, Butch. People are the same the world over. They just want to be understood."

"Right. I'll file that knowledge away in case I ever need it for encouragement."

Butch and Claire decided to take a room in a local bed and breakfast inn located in downtown Butler. There were only three commercial places to stay, and the bed and breakfast was much more charming and suited Butch and Claire better than the Holiday Inn Express and the Shady Oaks Motel, both located out on the bypass. The Jasmine House was located downtown, near the courthouse and library, and within walking distance to the county square where Sheriff Phillip's office was located. The sheriff had agreed to pay for their lodging and food expense while they were investigating the strange occurrences in his county. The Jasmine House was ideal for them and their work.

The Jasmine House had quite a colorful history, if one was to believe the stories that were being told to Butch and Claire as they interviewed the townspeople of Butler. According to legend, the house was rebuilt in 1890 by a local judge at that time. He was the circuit judge for a good portion of the old Choctaw Nations' area in Alabama, and he was one of those *horseback riding judges* that Claire had read about in so many novels as a young girl. If someone had offended or broken the law in one of his areas of responsibility, the local sheriff would incarcerate the suspect until the judge came riding into town to decipher who was right and who was in error. He meted out justice equally, according to the law as he understood it, but was never seen as a hanging judge. At the turn of the century, many judges and juries sentenced wrongdoers to the ultimate punishment—to hang from the end of a rope in the public square. Most of these judges were not soft on crime but were strong on reform. They would give most offenders, except for the crimes of murder or rape, a second chance to put their lives back on the path to good citizenship. They never gave anyone a third chance. In other words, they were fair, but firm in their decisions.

    The Jasmine House was first constructed around the time the city of Butler was incorporated and chosen as the county seat for Choctaw County. While the county was recognized as an official territory in 1819, the city of Butler was incorporated almost thirty years later. In 1848, it received its charter to form the city of Butler, and a year later a land baron and slave owner, Gossamer Hubbard bought the land and began the construction of his 'town house' in downtown Butler. Gossamer had been a railroad baron earlier in his life, following in the footsteps of his father. His grandfather had helped settle the area around Butler and was instrumental in gathering up the local Choctaw Nation people and ushering them out of the state on their way to Oklahoma. Gossamer was the wealthiest man south of the capital in Montgomery, and he spared no expense in the construction of his beloved Jasmine House. Everyone had large families in those early days, and the Hubbard families were no exception to that custom. Gossamer wanted his Jasmine House to be the gathering place for his extended family as well as his personal residence, so he built it in grandiose style. The residence had all the formal rooms on the first floor, with a root cellar and special hiding areas disguised as false walls in the basement. The house had three floors, eight bedrooms, all with their own inside plumbing and bathrooms, and the room above the main house was accessible only by a hidden staircase that appeared to go nowhere from the third floor of the mansion. If one knew where the secret latch was located, the upper room above the third floor could be entered from a permanent staircase. The *crow's nest*, as

Gossamer like to refer to his lofty hidden space, was large enough for a bedroom, bathroom, and kitchenette. In the late 1850s an early version of an elevator was added to the house for convenience. The walls and structure of the mansion could accommodate the installation of an elevator that would reach from the basement to the crow's nest, but the shaft could be hidden behind a plaster wall for privacy. Gossamer's Jasmine House was fully completed and available for occupancy in 1851, and the railroad baron enjoyed being the most influential person in Choctaw County until Butler was captured by the Yankees in 1864. Union Brigadier General James H. Wilson was ordered to lead a raid to destroy the arsenal at Selma, Alabama, and all other strongholds in the southwest portion of the state. The general invaded the city of Butler, but instead of burning it, he seized the Jasmine House as his headquarters, and he stayed there until the Treaty of Washington was signed, signaling the end of the American Civil War. He took his troops and moved north after the signing of that treaty, and the house reverted back to the estate of Gossamer Hubbard. Hubbard was killed in 1864 in a battle just a few miles north of his beloved Jasmine House, and he was buried in the family graveyard that was located just behind the mansion. The house remained in the family for many years, only to be sold at auction in the early 1960s for lack of payment of city, county, and state taxes. The Jasmine House was purchased for $75,000 by a local attorney and his wife, and immediately renovated as the only bed and breakfast inn within 50 miles of Butler. Looking at it as they pulled into the oversized circular drive in the front of the building, Claire thought it could have been constructed yesterday. It was pristine, pretty, and picturesque. She was excited to learn the history of the Jasmine House, and she loved the lavishness of the afternoon teas on the piazza, the herb garden in the rear of the lot, and the fourteen-foot ceilings in the bedroom she had been assigned to by the innkeeper. Butch had been assigned an adjoining room, and they planned to put the discreet doorway to use later that evening.

"Wow!" was all Claire could say as she flopped on the canopy bed, watching with delight as the ceiling fan far above her head turned slowly to keep the air circulating in her room. Butch had carried her overnight bags into the room for her, and he smiled down at the pretty young woman.

"You look like a little kid on her parent's bed," he laughed.

"Why don't you join me for a little nap?"

"A nap, huh?"

"Well, maybe a little more than a nap," she said, and gave him her most seductive glare.

"Later, Godiva!" Butch said as he sat her bags down on the floor and headed toward his own adjacent room.

"How do you know that I will be in the mood *later*?"

"I guess I'll have to take my chances. We have work to do right now." She sighed, rose from the bed, and began putting her clothes away in the dresser and closet. Butch was a lot of things, but spontaneous was not one of them.

"I want to freshen up a bit," she said as he moved out of her room. "I'll join you downstairs shortly." She washed her face, freshened her makeup, used the lavatory, and brushed through her long, blonde hair. If people had asked her a few years ago if she would be a private detective, sleuthing out hard criminals, packing a loaded firearm, and having a casual affair with her boss, she would have laughed in their faces. But here she was, and she was loving every minute of it! She took one final look at herself in the mirror and headed downstairs to meet Butch. He was sitting in a Victorian wing chair, looking over the local newspaper. He looked like a bull in a china shop—totally out of place.

"Are you ready to go?" he inquired as she casually walked down the elaborate and gracious staircase that led from the upper stories of the mansion.

"As ready as ever," she sighed. "Let's get this done so we can enjoy the ambiance of this marvelous mansion." Butch gave her one of his questionable glances, and they were off. Their first stop was at a small restaurant on the square. It was named Lulu's, but it looked nothing like the Lulu's in Gulf Shores. This was a simple diner, and nothing more. They took a seat at a sidewalk table and watched as an overweight waitress approached their table. Her nametag identified her as Lulu.

"Are you the famous Lulu of Choctaw County?" Butch asked the tired-looking woman.

"I imagine I'm the *only* Lulu in Choctaw County," she answered with a smile."

"Are you related to the Lulu in Gulf Shores, the sister of the famous country singer?"

"Nah. I doubt it. If I were related to someone famous with any money at all I would move out of this godforsaken area of the state." Without further comment about her family tree, Lulu asked what they wanted to drink.

"Just water for both of us," Butch said. He knew ordering unsweetened tea in Butler would be like trying to get a proper Chablis wine for a nice piece of fish at dinner. It simply wasn't worth the trouble to hear the story again about "The only kind of tea we have here is sweetened." There were many differences from one small town to the other in the deep South, but outside the city limits of the larger cities, the availability of unsweetened tea was like trying to find a dinosaur's tooth.

"OK, Hun," she said in her deep southern drawl. "Have you decided on what you want for lunch?"

"What do you recommend?" Claire asked.

"Well, I made fresh chicken and dumplings this morning. If you like that kind of thing, my recipe is considered the best in the area. We serve green beans and cornbread with it, and some apple cobbler for dessert."

"Sounds wonderful," Butch said. "Make it for two." Claire nodded her approval, and Lulu waddled off toward her kitchen.

"This has to be the most original country restaurant within 50 miles of Butler," Claire said. "I'll bet the food is scrumptious!"

"I imagine all the restaurants in these parts of the county are like Lulu's. These local folks wouldn't tolerate poorly prepared food. And I'll bet the beans and chickens didn't come from a local grocery store."

"I wouldn't take that bet for any reason!" Claire said. "These are *real* people Butch, with nothing but the truth and facts of life abounding."

"You sound like a poet, or a philosopher."

"They are as my father used to say, 'The salt of the Earth.'" Their lunch plates were brought to the table, steaming and smelling wonderful, and they dug into the best cooking in Choctaw County.

* * *

After lunch Butch called Lulu over to their table. He wanted to compliment her on her restaurant's cooking, and he also wanted to learn how receptive she might be to answering some questions about the local area.

"Lulu," Butch asked, "how long have you lived in Butler?" She must have thought it was a silly question because she began to laugh as she answered.

"All my life. I was born at home, and that's about all there was to it."

"Did your mother have a doula or a midwife?" Claire asked.

"What's a doula? I know what a midwife is, but we couldn't afford any additional help when I came along. The local doctor came by the house after my birth to help with things and to help prevent my mother getting an infection."

"A doula is someone who is licensed to advise a woman during her pregnancy, but she doesn't actually deliver the baby. A midwife basically delivers the baby when a hospital is not nearby for the event."

"We didn't have any of that. My grandmother helped my mom, my grandfather wrote all the particulars into the family Bible, and that was it." Lulu began to gather up the dishes at their table.

"Do you mind sharing with us when you were born?"

"According to grandpa's entry into the Bible, I was born on August 21st, 1955. He called the county courthouse and reported the birth, and that was all that was required at that time. A good many women today use midwives, but it wasn't a popular thing to do when I was born."

"I guess that means that no one would have reported any injuries to a local doctor if they had been confronted by an unusual person or animal in the woods."

"What kind of animal?" Lulu asked. She was beginning to look questioningly at the two newcomers.

"I'll get back to that. Do you mind telling us your last name?"

"Nelson. Why, who's asking?"

"No one in particular, Lulu. I know this is your busy time, with lunch and all the meals you serve to your loyal customers. Do you mind if we come back after the rush and talk a little more about local things?" Butch asked. Lulu wasn't sure how to answer, but she agreed.

"Make it after 3:00 PM. We can take a table in the back for a little bit if you have more questions. Oh, by the way. I come from a long line of Nelsons, going back to the Trail of Tears in the mid-1800s. Now, that was a tragedy!" Turning away from their table, Lulu mumbled that she would see them at 3:00 PM, and then she disappeared into the kitchen. Butch and Claire got up from the table and headed outside.

"We need to think outside of the box on this case, Butch. Many of these people probably don't go to the doctor regularly, a lot of them were probably born at home or somewhere other than a hospital, and they don't see things in the same light as we do."

"I understand your concern. How can we make them feel more comfortable when we are questioning them?" Butch asked.

"I read this novel by MW Burdette, and he said that not enough people were in the 'people business,' and that's why it's difficult to breach divides of culture and historic differences in people."

"People Business? What the hell is the people business?"

"It's making people feel included, safe, and comfortable around you before you begin to grill them on the subject you need to discuss with them. *Make a friend, and then make the sale* was one of the quotes he used often in his book."

"Is that why you were questioning Lulu about her birth and early family life in Butler? I wasn't sure where you were going with that logic, nor why you were pursuing it."

"Butch, people tend to talk more freely with people whom they identify with. Sure, authority figures can coax some information from people from time to time, but people share *everything* with their friends. And while we can't honestly befriend everyone in Butler and Choctaw County in a matter of a few days, the more they like us, the more they will trust us."

"That makes sense. I'll try to be more empathetic in the future." Butch said. Claire smiled her million-dollar smile at him, and they got back into the pickup truck.

Chapter 5

Local Rumors

Every small town in Alabama had stories that were larger than life, and Butler was no exception. The difference in the stories in Butler was that this was Choctaw County, the original home of the Choctaw Tribe of Native Americans. While the larger population of Choctaw Indians were located in middle-Mississippi, the Choctaw Nation in Alabama was centered in the Butler area. Native American tribes passed their stories along through storytelling from one generation to the next, much like the Jewish culture kept its culture alive for thousands of years. Whether or not the stories were embellished as they were being shared with the younger generations is not something that can be measured accurately. However, if there were any stories about an invisible cult operating in Choctaw County, many of them would be believed by the general population. The culture of the county was secretive, at best. Early in the 1960s when integration of the African American children was introduced into the local schools, the local grand dragon of the Klu Klux Klan took his membership underground to fight against what they considered was a government takeover of the schools. There had already been discrimination between the white folks and the Native American locals who were direct dependents of those who had to vacate their lands and move to Oklahoma during the Trail of Tears. The Klu Klux Klan seized upon the opportunity to drive a wedge between the Choctaw Native descendants and the white population, siding with them as being discriminated against as well with their stories of the Carpet Baggers who abused their survivors of the Civil War. Over a period of several years, a strong bond was made between the descendants of the Choctaw Nation and the Klu Klux Klan. What made things even stranger was that both groups visibly disappeared from public view. It was suggested that they operated in the shadows, away from public eyes, and solely for the benefit of disrupting the local government and all organized businesses. That's basically what the sheriff had suggested, but there was no hard and fast proof. Butch and Claire hoped that Lulu, and others like her, could shed some necessary light on the subject so they could either prove or disprove a cultic existence in Choctaw County. They would know soon if Lulu would confide in them, assuming she had something to disclose on the subject. Claire and Butch had a couple of hours to kill, so they thought that they would just walk around the small downtown area of Butler to get a better feel for the locals.

"Butch, are those two people sitting on the park bench on the courthouse lawn staring at us?" Claire asked.

"Claire, *everyone* is staring at us," he laughed.

"Why?"

"Because we are outsiders, interlopers, spies, and probably up to no good!"

"We are not!" she protested.

"To these people, anyone whom they don't know could be the enemy. When you think of Ashburn you recall the local people in town, most of which are reasonably trusting of the police and other authorities. However, if you drive just a few miles into the countryside, like Pea Ridge or other small communities, they don't trust us anymore than these people in Butler trust us. It's just the way things are, and that type of thinking cannot be changed overnight."

"How do we suggest that we change that dynamic? If we can't get them to open up to us, we won't be able to help Sheriff Phillips, and that won't please our boss back in Ashburn."

"I'm trying to decide the best way to proceed, but I think I agree with your suggestion of befriending as many of the locals as possible. Do you have a gut feeling if having Sheriff Phillips introduce us to various groups is good or weakens our argument?"

"In my experience, empathy can work miracles when one wants to get close to another person. If we can find a way to get the locals to trust us by making them believe we are just like them, we will have a much greater impact on the investigation. The problem as I see it is that I have no idea of how to accomplish that goal!"

"Let's look for obvious sighting of physical things that might lend us the impression that either the KKK or the descendants of Choctaw tribesmen are present in modern-day Butler." She agreed, and they continued their slow-paced walk throughout the city square, the main downtown shops, and the adjacent streets and businesses that peppered the downtown area of Butler. After an hour they headed back towards Lulu's, but they wanted to stop by the sheriff's office first to discuss how he might help them. They stopped at Tallulah Ashalintubbi's desk and asked if the sheriff would see them. She called up to his office and he agreed. The sheriff did not get up from behind his desk when they came into his office, but he motioned them to the two chairs in front of his desk.

"Sheriff, Claire and I would like to ask you to introduce us to some people this afternoon, if your schedule will allow it. We were hoping to talk to some of the older folks in Butler, and if you have a retirement home or other facility similar to that, we might be able to get that done before the end of the day."

"Sure, let's plan on it. What time would you like to speak to them?"

"Maybe 4:00 PM. Will that work for you?"

"Yes, but anything after that will run into their dinnertime, and they will not be cooperative. Why would you want to speak to older folks first? Many of them have been confined in their apartments for years, and they haven't circulated in the general population for a while."

"What we have discovered over the years is that older folks and children are the most honest when questioned about specific events. That doesn't mean that we don't trust what young adults and middle-aged folks have to say, but children don't readily know how to lie, and older folks don't really care what most people think about them once they are pushed aside by society," Claire said,

"I've never thought about things that way, but I can see your point. I'll call over to Sunset Hills and let them know that we will be visiting around 4:00 PM. Do you want to meet me there or for us to go together in one car?"

"We'll meet you there, Sheriff," Butch said. "Just give us the directions."

"That's easy," he said. He pointed out of his big window overlooking the square and told them the only five-story building in town was Sunset Hills Senior Living Center.

"Is it a government supported facility?"

"No, but the rents are controlled by the government, so just about anyone with any income can qualify to live there. We have very few homeless people on our public streets in Butler," the Sheriff smiled. Shaking his hand warmly once more, Butch and Claire left his office for Lulu's once more.

* * *

Butch and Claire could hardly recognize Lulu's once they entered at 3:00 PM. The once heavily crowded restaurant at noon was totally abandoned, with the exception of a young boy busing tables, the cook who was visible through the kitchen serving window, and Lulu. She was standing at the old-fashioned cash register counting the money the restaurant had taken in for the day. As they approached her, she nodded at them, but she kept counting and mumbling the numbers under her breath.

"Aren't you afraid someone might try to rob you of your money?" Claire asked Lulu. Without verbally answering, because Lulu was still tabulating her cash drawer, she pointed to a snub-nosed .38 caliber revolver in open view on the bottom shelf of the small hostess stand.

"Do you know how to use that gun?" Butch asked. Having finally finished counting the days money total, Lulu spoke for the first time since they had returned to her restaurant.

"That revolver solves two purposes. Anyone who might think of robbing me knows that they might get shot, and they have no idea how good a shot I am. So, it is a deterrent for most people who might think of doing something crazy. I've never had to use it here at the restaurant."

"Do you know how to shoot accurately?" Claire asked. Lulu smiled before she answered.

"I grew up on a dirt road with the nearest house being a half-a-mile away from us. I had three sisters and no brothers to protect us when our parents were working long days at the mill or the railroad yard. I was the oldest, so my father took me out back in the woods and taught me how to handle a pistol, shotgun, and 30-30 rifle. I won't say I'm a great shot, but I killed my share of rabbits and deer, and I'm really accurate up to twenty yards or less, so I would say the revolver alone is not a threat, but he shooter as well!" Lulu smiled again after telling her story.

"That's good to know," Butch laughed. "Remind us not to spook you when you're counting your money!" Everyone laughed at that comment. "Have you got a minute to talk to us now?"

"Sure. Come on back and we'll sit at that table near the kitchen." On her way to the back of the restaurant, Lulu flipped the Open/Closed sign over on the door, turned the thumb lock on the door, and took off her stained apron. "Can I get you some coffee or anything while we talk? The coffee is fresh."

"That would be nice," Claire said, beginning to get sleepy after that big meal at lunch. "Just black for both of us," Claire added. Lulu poured out three cups of coffee in white ceramic mugs that had *Lulu's* stenciled on the sides. Somehow bringing all three cups and a pot to replenish their coffee when needed, Lulu sat down at the table with them.

"How do you do that?" Claire asked Lulu when she joined them.

"Do What?"

"I can barely carry two cups of coffee, much less three and a coffee pot at one time. I've always marveled at the ability of a good server to handle so many dishes at one time, and you definitely have that touch." Butch immediately knew that Claire was trying to mimic the principles that MW Burdette's book had mentioned about getting to know people better before grilling them on any facts one wanted to reveal.

"Shoot, Honey. I've been waitressing almost all my life. I started at Alice's Café when I was fourteen years old and started this restaurant when my late husband and I had been married only a few years. He's been gone ten years now, but he was my cook, and I ran the frontend. I have been known to carry six full plates of food at one time."

"Have you ever dropped anything?"

"I guess I did in the beginning when I was learning how to do it. However, I haven't dropped anything in years. You have to remember if I drop a plate of food, that's my profit for several hours of the day. There's not much markup in food. We don't server liquor or beer, so my margins are much less than some other restaurants."

"We didn't notice any places in town which advertised that they served alcohol. I'm guess this is a dry county?" Claire's statement brought another chuckle from Lulu.

"Well, we've got the bootleggers and moonshine stills, but there's no *legal* alcohol sold in Choctaw County. If you know where to get it, and you're willing to chance not getting poisoned or arrested for taking the chance, you can get alcohol in Butler!"

"Why do you think the county is still dry when so many counties all around you allow the sale and serving of alcohol?" Butch asked.

"Bootleggers and Baptist Church members are the main reason," Lulu answered. Claire's expression let Lulu know that she didn't have a clue what Lulu was saying. "The Baptist Church members are encouraged by their pastors and deacons to vote down the alcohol provisions for ethical reasons, and the bootleggers want to keep their demand high for the illegal alcohol that they are cooking up in the hills around Butler." Claire just shook her head in amusement.

"Anyway, that's why I try to not drop plates full of food!" was Lulu's last comment about her abilities to carry more than one or two plates at time without them crashing to the restaurant floor. The explanation seemed sufficient for Claire and Butch. "I know you didn't want to come back to talk to me about my café and how I operate it, so how can I help you?"

"Lulu, I know you've lived in Butler all of your life, and you probably know as much about this town and Choctaw County as anyone living here. We have heard rumors of an association between remnants of the old KKK organization and the Choctaw Indian nation, at least of those Native American who stayed behind and didn't join in the Trail of Tears march to Oklahoma. We know that there is historical proof that some of those early Choctaw Indians stayed behind and melded into the local population, living in the woods and surrounding areas of Butler. We understand how a proud nation of Native Americans could have felt betrayed by their newly arriving European neighbors and revoted against being moved off their historical homeland. The rumors further suggest that the remnants of the Choctaw Nation have formed an alliance with another sect of people who also believe they were betrayed when the U.S. Government demanded that they give up their slaves, and then were treated horribly by Carpetbaggers who took unfair advantage of a defeated

South after the Civil War. That sect I'm referring to is the KKK, or some splinter group of the overall organization. While this scenario seems possible, it also seems rather fantastic to embrace," Claire said.

"So, what are you actually asking?" Lulu said. "Do I believe the rumors, or have I seen any evidence of such an alliance?"

"Something like that," Butch said. "With Claire and I having lived in the South all of our lives, we know a lot about the KKK, and their efforts back in the 1950s and 1960s to stifle the inevitable arrival of equal rights for all races of people. Many people thought that the KKK was only protesting the interaction of blacks and whites, when the true beliefs of the Klu Klux Klan were that any impurity that would be caused by intermarriage between the races was unacceptable. You probably can see why we were a little surprised when we were told that a Native American remnant of people would form an alliance between themselves and the KKK." Lulu didn't speak for a moment, and when she did, she was very careful with her words.

"Please don't quote me on this, but I personally believe that the KKK had the same kind of purpose that Adolf Hitler had when he was rounding up and murdering all of the Jews in Europe. The KKK members down here believe that they are a superior race to the African American population, and while they aren't necessarily suggesting that all black people should be killed, they do not approve nor forgive the intermarriage of any of the races, particularly the blacks and the whites. That's the attitude that I've grown up with in Butler, and it hasn't changed since I was a little girl. So, do I think the Choctaws and the KKK could be trying to unite to fight against the U.S. Government? The answer is yes!"

"Do you know of any instances lately where that kind of thing has been mentioned by anyone whose eaten in your café?"

"I have the same attitude as Las Vegas. 'What goes on at Lulu's, stays at Lulu's,'" she said with a smile. I can tell you this much. There are people in this town who hate every person with any heritage of Choctaw blood, and also a similar situation with African Americans. One thing I will admit to, though, and I think it's a little odd," she said.

"What?" Butch fished for Lulu to continue her admission.

"I've seen blacks fight blacks, and I've seen whites fight whites, and I've seen blacks fight whites, but I have never seen blacks fight Choctaws. If you think about it, that's a little odd, don't you agree?" Claire and Butch were nodding while Lulu was making her observation, as if they agreed with every word she was saying.

"If we were to start talking to people about our suspicions and the rumors that we've been hearing, who should we go about asking folks to verify or deny the rumors?" This question from Butch drew a big smile from Lulu.

"Do either of you gamble?" Lulu asked. Claire again looked at Butch for some sign of understanding why Lulu was changing the subject.

"Nothing serious," Butch said. "Why?"

"Because if you were a serious gambler, you'd always know the odds of winning before you placed a bet. For instance, Blackjack has the best odds for a player to win, which is only one percent less than the house. From there the odds move more in favor of the house and away from the person placing the bet. For instance, for Craps the odds are almost 50-50 that you will win or lose. Roulette is less favorable for one to win against the house, and the slot machines are the worst odds in the entire casino to try and increase your money."

"You seem to know a lot about gambling, Lulu. Is there a storyline there?" Claire asked with a smile. Lulu returned the smile, and she looked a little devilish doing so. When she answered, Claire and Butch were amazed at the confession that Lulu made.

"I neglected to tell you about a little adventure I took when I first graduated from high school. I knew I didn't have the money or the grades to go to college, and there were no scholarships or loans I qualified for since I was single and had no real job. So, being young, inexperience, and daring, I packed a small suitcase and hitchhiked to Las Vegas. Because I was under the age of twenty-one, I was not allowed to work on the casino floor, serve drinks, or do anything else which would require an identification card or driver's license proving my age. I started out in one of the kitchens, slept at the YWCA at night, and eventually was able to acquire a fake ID that showed I was twenty-one years old. At that point, I was able to get a job serving drinks to gamblers as they played the various games of chance throughout the casino."

"Which one?" Claire asked.

"Harrah's had just opened in 1973, and they were hiring lots of young women to work the floor, and I got lucky. That began a short, but profitable, run for me in Vegas. It didn't last long, and I was back in Butler within a year of getting my first Vegas job." Butch was surprised that this matronly-appearing woman had ever been attractive enough to land a job in Vegas, much less stay there long enough to learn about the odds of the games of chance.

"You definitely are a woman of mystery," Claire said. "Why did you return to Butler? I would have thought that once you were able to get away from such a small, confining town, that you would have wanted to stay away."

"I missed home, and I had had a little success, so that's when I decided to move back and start my own restaurant. I knew how to cook and how to run a restaurant, so I took a chance and started Lulu's. I met my husband, Larry Smith, at a church social, we married the next spring, and we lived together forty years until he died a couple of years ago. I've had a pretty good life," she said with a smile.

"What did you mean when said 'We should know the odds of winning before we placed a bet?" Claire asked.

"Most people in Butler, Alabama, were born here, grew up here, and have never left. A few have gone off to college for a degree or for law school, but most have not. They are simple people with clear-cut goals and very little imagination. I'm not saying this to be cruel or harsh, but it's simply the truth. My experiences in Las Vegas opened my eyes to a lot of things, and I'm not nearly as suspicious of strangers as most of them are. You just need to pick carefully those you wish to question so you don't gain a reputation of 'working for the man,' if you know what I mean." Butch could see a golden opportunity opening up for them, so he pressed Lulu for help.

"Lulu, you know these people better than we could ever learn about them in a few short days or weeks if we had that kind of time to stay in Butler, which we don't. Could you help direct us to a few people who might be able to tell us what they know about the rumors of the KKK and

Choctaw Nation survivors who might be plotting against the county, state, and the U.S. Government?" Lulu looked skeptical at first, then she began to nod her head.

"I can't promise you anything, Mr. Todd, but I will put on my thinking cap and try to come up with a few names for you. Off the top of my head, I know that Pastor Smith at the Butler Lutheran Church might be willing to share an incident that he had a few weeks back. He was so shaken by it that he preached a special sermon on loving one's neighbor as oneself. I'll try to think of some more for you to speak to as well."

"You mentioned that his name was Pastor Smith? Any relationship to you or your husband Larry?"

"My husband's cousin, but they weren't close. Larry was not much of a church goer, and I went to services alone most of the time, except for Christmas and Easter. Larry was a good man, but not much of a 'Bible-thumper,' she said."

"You might want to go by the church and see if you can catch the pastor there because he is usually in the office on Mondays. In the meantime, I'll try to come up with a few more names for you." Lulu got up from the table, indicating that she was through talking for the present time, but both Claire and Butch had learned much more than they ever thought possible from the owner of a local café." They got ready to leave, Claire thanked Lulu and gave her a little hug, and she and Jonathan were out the door and headed for the Lutheran Church.

Chapter 6

Facts or Fiction?

When Butch and Claire had investigated in other cities where they didn't know much about the local population or the customs in that area, they had to rely on journals, newspaper articles, and other historical data to give them the overall attitude and atmosphere of the area. Nothing was foolproof, but one could get a pretty good glimpse into the minds of the residents of an area since history almost always repeated itself when customs and habits of the local population rarely changed in the short term. When they were investigating the murder of the two professor's deaths at Ashburn University a couple of years ago, both Butch and Claire were so familiar with the area, the townsfolk, and the customs of Ashburn that it was easier performing surveillance, asking questions of local residents, and getting a real feeling for the facts in the case than it had been when they worked the case of the crash of the C5A cargo plane in Charleston, South Carolina. They succeeded anyway, though the task seemed impossible at times. They would just have to suck it up and overcome any unknowns that might normally deter them from their goals. One of the things in their favor now was the fact that they had an "inside person" working alongside them, making the possibility of success greater than if they were slamming their heads against a stone wall. Whether or not there could be enough leads from Lulu Smith to solve the case was yet to be determined. As they pulled up in front of the beautiful but small Lutheran Church building, Butch noticed that there was an automobile parked in the pastor's space, and his spirits were immediately lifted.

"Let's see if the good pastor is in," Butch said as he exited his pickup truck. Claire opened her door and joined him as he approached the side door to the building marked "Office." They knocked on the door, but no one answered, so Butch turned the doorknob and discovered that it was not locked. Looking at Claire with a questioning smile, Butch stepped through the door and into the hallway that ran the length of the administration wing of the church. They saw a light on in an office at the end of the hallway, and they headed toward it and someone playing a piano. When they got to the door, they saw a man in his mid-forties wearing a set of Bose headphones with his eyes closed. He was playing the piano, listening to something on his headphones, and humming along with the music. Butch had heard of multi-tasking, but he had never seen anything quite like this. After standing in his presence for a few minutes, Pastor Smith must have sensed the presence of his visitors because he slowly opened his eyes, stopped playing the piano, and cleared his throat.

"I'm sorry," the pastor said. "Did we have an appointment this afternoon?"

"No, Pastor Smith, but Claire Cavendish and I would like to ask you a few questions, if that's OK," Jonathan asked. Pastor Smith looked around and saw Claire standing behind Butch, and he welcomed both of them to take a chair near the piano.

"I'm just preparing for the service on Wednesday, and it calms my spirits if I play the piano while I listen to my prepared remarks which I have previously recorded. I guess that looked strange to you."

"Actually, it looked awesome," Claire said. "I don't remember ever seeing something like that in the past."

"Just my own little technique of preparation. Do either of you attend church regularly?" Now the shoe was on the other foot, and Pastor Smith was doing the inquiring. While neither of them was a regular attendee of any particular church, they didn't consider themselves pagans either. Claire had grown up in the Roman Catholic Church, while Butch had belonged to the Ashburn Baptist Church that he had attended with his parents when he was growing up in the small city of Ashburn. Life had driven a wedge between both Claire and her Roman Catholic faith, and Butch just didn't get around to regularly attending services anymore. They weren't agnostics, but they weren't engaged either.

"Both Claire and I have been affiliated with churches in our past, but we're not overly active at the present time." The pastor smiled and just nodded his head in acknowledgement of the facts. He had done his job inquiring about these two people's church attendance, and he didn't feel responsible to proselyte them into his own congregation.

"What brings you into my church today? It obviously isn't marriage counseling or your desire to join our congregation," the pastor said. Claire thought that this guy didn't beat around the bush either.

"We were visiting with Lulu Smith after a great lunch at her café, and she told us that you might have some insight into the possible rumors going around concerning the KKK and the Choctaw Nation." Rather than lead the pastor to the answer they wanted, they both said nothing until he had answered Butch's question. They wanted to know if he would open up about the incident Lulu had mentioned which had occurred in his church service.

"I'm guessing Lulu said something about the little altercation in the service a few weeks ago. It was rather innocent, but I can't deny that it didn't happen."

"Pastor, what exactly happened? Were there any physical threats or punches thrown?" Ronald Smith looked uncomfortable when he denied anything serious happening, but he did admit that he had asked the troublemaker to leave the service.

"Do you remember his name?" Claire asked.

"I do, but we treat conversations between parishioners and us as sacred, much like a physician," Pastor Smith said, playing the confidentially card. He was hoping that would be the end of this line of questioning, but he didn't know anything about Claire's tenacity. She was nodding as he spoke, giving him a false impression that she was going to yield to his privacy explanation.

"Pastor Smith, may I ask you something just to clarify my thinking?"

"Of course, Ms. Cavendish, what is it?"

"If you suspected ahead of time that someone in your congregation might come back after services with a high-powered rifle and begin executing people, wouldn't you have a legal and moral obligation to bring that information to the attention of the local police department?" Not wishing to get trapped by his own slick explanation of things, he simply said that he would alert the authorities in such a case.

"If you take the current suspected relationship in Butler between the members of the KKK and the remnant of the Choctaw Nation, would you want to be held morally, and possibly legally, liable for not coming forward and sharing all you know with us. We have been instructed by the sheriff's department to help him get to the root of the racial stresses now existing between Butler's white citizens and a possible coalition between the Choctaw Indians and the militarized wing of the KKK. I am assuming that you're aware of the missing status of Judge Louis Doran. He has been missing for more than six weeks. Supposedly he was killed at home, but the last people reported to have seen him are associates of the KKK and the Choctaw Nation. You wouldn't be betraying a trust to inform us who made those demands in your church service. It's really just a matter of public record. Unfortunately, we were not around when the disclosures were initially made, so we need someone to bring us up to speed on what happened. Will you not at least do that for us and for the city of Butler? It might help us keep this situation from getting out of control." Butch thought that Claire had missed her calling. She should have either gone into aluminum siding or encyclopedia sales. She was a terrific closer. The only question left was whether she would be convincing enough to sway Pastor Smith's conscious. Smith hesitated, then he spoke.

"I probably should not share this information with you two outsiders, but the last thing we need in this small town is a revolution or the second-coming of the Civil War." Once he had decided to cooperate with them, he couldn't stop talking. There was no order to his sentences, so Claire stopped him momentarily to ask him to start from the beginning, taking each instance as they had happened.

"The thing about being a pastor in a Christian oriented church is that we have to be colorblind and do our best to not hold a grudge against any person of any race, religion, creed, nationality, or any other distinguishing characterization which would single that person out to be different from the masses. Contrary to the beliefs of many protestant churches around the world, Jesus was Asian or of

Mediterranean descent. Jews are not white, and His birth mother was definitely Jewish, as she was a descendant from the House of David, the second king of the Israelites around the year 1000 BC. Neither was he black, as He is often portrayed in churches in South America and the Southern United States. The importance of His origin was that He told us the important things where we should focus was on the life after this one on Earth. I'm not trying to preach to you, but those are the facts that we read about in the New Testament of the Holy Bible in the first four books, commonly named the gospels, and in the final book of the Bible, Revelation."

"I'm not minimizing nor disputing your points, Pastor, but what has that got to do with what you can tell us about the recent incident in your church service?" Butch asked. Pastor Smith looked at Butch sympathetically, knowing that he would probably not fully understand the parable of the Good Samaritan either.

"May I call you Butch and Claire?"

"Absolutely," they both responded at the same time.

"Butch, people will tell a physician, an attorney, and a preacher many things they will not tell a family member or one of their best friends. A few weeks ago, one of my parishioners came to me in confidence stating that she knew of a murder that had taken place recently. She wanted me to know, mostly to relieve her feeling of guilt of not having shared that information with Sheriff Conrad Phillips' office. She swore me to secrecy, and at that time there were no reports of anyone missing or any bodies discovered that had been murdered. A week or so later the possible remains of Judge Julius Malone's body was found in an abandoned creek bed by some hunters out in the woods tracking and trying to kill a deer. When the authorities had the body moved to the morgue, the autopsy showed that the judge had been tortured sexually, and then hung from the neck until dead. Once dead, his body was thrown into the open ditch as a sign of disrespect. I should have come forward and told the sheriff's office about my knowledge of the kidnapping and murder shared by my congregant."

"Why didn't you eventually come forward once the murder was public knowledge?" Claire asked.

"I figured it was too late to help the judge, and I had an obligation to my church member to keep her confidence, or at least I thought that I did. Now, I'm not so sure."

"Is there anything else you're not sharing," Claire asked? Once a person revealed to Claire that they could not be trusted with being honest in a past situation, she didn't trust them with future opportunities either.

"What makes you say that?" Paster Smith asked. He looked guilty to Claire just because she no longer could believe anything that came out of his mouth. Butch and Claire said nothing, and the pressure of silence, along with his guilty conscience, were the factors that revealed that there was more to his omissions than just what his congregant had shared with him. "You people don't understand. If I say anything else, people may die!"

"What people?" Butch asked.

"I've already said too much," he began to protest. "I can't say anything else." Paster Smith became quiet, and it initially appeared that their meeting with him was over. The preacher rose from his chair and began walking toward the door. The only problem was that Claire and Butch had remained in their chairs without any intention of leaving until they got all the information that they had come to the Butler Lutheran Church for. Realizing that his guests had not risen from their chairs, the pastor came back to them and pleaded with them to leave.

"Pastor Smith, do you understand what obstruction of justice is and what penalties are levied against anyone who misrepresents or stands in the way of important information being revealed to the court? In this case, it would be up to Judge Louis Doran to exercise his judgement as to whether or not you have committed such a crime," Butch said. Pastor Smith looked like a deer caught in the headlights of an automobile just before being hit on the highway. He had never thought about the possibility that he was voluntarily committing a crime.

"I haven't purposely misled the judge on anything. I simply didn't reveal information that I was given by a member of my congregation. There was no intent there."

"I guess that would be up to the prosecuting attorney and the court to decide, wouldn't it? If they decide you withheld important information, you might only be charged with criminal negligence, which is a misdemeanor. Usually, a misdemeanor in the state of Alabama is punishable by a hefty fine and probation. Of course, that would go on your permanent record as well. However, if the judge decides to hold you to a higher standard, that of obstruction of justice and criminal conspiracy, which is considered a felony, punishable with up to five years in prison, a fine, and a bad mark against your record. It's up to you but having spent a little time with Judge Doran today, I don't know if I would want to roll the dice, if you know what I mean." Now, Pastor Smith had sat down, was visibly shaking, and perspiration had visibly broken out on his face. It was evident to Claire and Butch that they had Pastor Smith right where they wanted him.

"Let's try this again, Pastor Smith," Claire said. "What else do you know or suspect that we should know?"

Chapter 7

Revelation

There weren't many times in Claire's life when she felt uncomfortable putting a person of interest under the scrutiny of severe questioning. If a person was holding out information that they needed to solve a case, then it was perfectly acceptable to squeeze the uncooperative party a bit to get the desired results. However, blackmailing a man of the cloth was stretching the level of comfort under any circumstances. She and Butch would simply wait and see what the pastor had to say before they made any more demands of him. It would be obvious to anyone but a totally blind person that the good reverend was uncomfortable talking about one of his parishioners, but Claire and Butch pushed on with their questions.

"You mentioned one of your parishioners, right? Was it a man or a woman who approached you?" Butch asked once more.

"That's where things get messy," Pastor Smith answered. "The person who spoke to me and swore me to silence was a woman who had seen her husband do some pretty bad things to Judge Malone. She told me that the men who were torturing him were upset that the judge had ruled in favor of a half breed over that of a white man."

"And her husband was one of the men who tortured and murdered the judge?" Claire asked.

"Oh, no! Nothing like that. Her husband belongs to a special lodge where they teach that it is against the will of God to marry outside of your race, religion, or creed. It could have been a black man who was convicted, instead of the white man, and the outcome would have been the same."

"Tell us more about this so-called lodge to which her husband is a member," Butch said.

"That's the problem. I don't know much more than I've already told you. You would have to speak to her, and if I give you her name, she will know that I have betrayed her trust." Claire thought for a moment and spoke carefully to make sure she didn't offend or turn off Pastor Smith.

"Why don't you give us her name, and we will find a way to confront her without her knowing you shared that information with us?" Claire offered.

"How would you do that without just lying to her and misleading her as to your interest in speaking to her?" Pastor Smith asked.

"You should let us worry about things like that, Pastor. Look, we must speak to someone who has inside knowledge of the cult practices going on in Choctaw County. Otherwise, we will never discover enough information to determine how to interrupt the carnage going on here in Butler and the surrounding area," Claire said. Claire saw that her pleas had persuaded Pastor Smith to share some information about his church member, if not everything.

"The man whose wife approached me is Leroy Smithson. Her name is Ruby, and they have been members of my church for many years. They were married in my church by a previous minister over twenty years ago. They are upstanding members of the town of Butler, and neither of them have ever been involved in any unlawful act." Claire thought, *until now*, but didn't say the words out loud.

"Where can we find Leroy and Ruby? Do they live in town?" Butch asked.

"No, they live a few miles out of town in a remote area of the county. They live in an unusual community, so you'd better call her before you just drop by. People have been shot for showing up unannounced at homes in Choctaw County. They tend to shoot first and ask questions later," the minister said.

"Thanks for the heads up. We'll be careful," Claire said.

"And you won't tell them that I sent you. Right?"

"We're old hands at disguise, Pastor," Butch said and gave him a wink. "They'll never know you were the source of our information."

"Good, because Leroy has a mean streak. He's beaten Ruby and the kids before, and I don't want him coming after me."

"You'll be fine, Pastor," Claire reassured him as they turned and left the Lutheran Church. Claire waited until they were back in the pickup truck before she asked her next question. "Do you think we should get Sheriff Phillips and his people involved in our visit to the Smithson home?"

"Are you thinking that a local won't shoot at the sheriff or his deputies?"

"It never hurts to be cautious, Butch. I know as a fighter pilot that's not in your DNA, but we might want to stop and think about those things." Butch purposely sat looking at Claire before starting up the engine of his truck. After a few minutes of total silence Butch gave her his answer.

"Yes, but no," he said and turned over the ignition. The truck started up and Butch put it in reverse so they could head back to The Jasmine House for dinner and their evening's stay in Butler.

"I'm confused, Butch. Yes, but no? What does that even mean?" he smiled at her before he gave her his explanation.

"It means, 'Yes,' we should think about it, which I did. The 'No,'' means we should proceed as planned. For all we know the sheriff may be in the same fraternal organization as Leroy and the other rednecks in town."

"Do you think that he would have gone out of his way to have mayor Hannity send us over to assist him if he were part of the conspiracy? Does that make a lot of sense to you?"

"None of this makes a lot of sense to me, but I'd rather ask for forgiveness than permission. Forgiveness can't be turned down, but only ignored and unappreciated. Permission can get doors slammed into ones faces. See my logic?"

"I see your point, but I'm not sure that I agree. If we are kind and nice to the locals perhaps they will open up to us and help us solve our problem."

"I don't want this response to you to sound rude, but aren't you being a little naïve thinking that if someone is involved in the kidnapping and murder of a judge that they will come out and confess to their crimes?"

"It has probably happened before," she tried to defend her undefendable statement.

"Do you remember when we were playing cards at the casino in Montgomery and I told you to not try to get the nine card, but you ignored me and lost the big pile of money on the table?" Claire blanched a little remembering how mad Butch got at the time.

"I remember. What's the big deal, and how does it relate to our situation now?"

"The card hand you were holding was the jack, ten of clubs, eight of diamonds, and seven of clubs. If you had drawn the nine of any suits, you would have won twice the amount of money which was on the table at that time, and I remember the amount was several hundred dollars. That run of cards is considered a simple 'straight,' and it beats most of the other hands anyone could have had on the table."

"So, what did I do wrong?"

"You were *drawing to an inside straight*, and that's one of the hardest things to do with success. The only card that can get you a win is a nine of any suite. However, if you had kept the jack, and drawn four new cards you might have gotten one or two pairs of cards, and I remember the winner of that hand won with a pair of tens."

"What does that have to do with us asking the sheriff to accompany us to the Smithson's?"

"The odds that the sheriff doesn't have some connection to the fraternal organization or some of the men in that club would be like drawing to an inside strait. Understand my logic?"

"No, but we'll do it your way. Then, if we blow the whole thing, I can blame our failure on you!" Claire said with a pout.

"I'll take my chances," Butch said, and unexpectedly gave her a peck on the cheek.

"What's that for?" Claire asked. "Are you trying to make up?"

"No, it's not that. I just think you're too cute when you pout like that." Claire cut her eyes at him and then looked out the window. She didn't speak to him again until they arrived at the bed and breakfast inn.

They pulled up in front of The Jasmine House Inn and Claire's spirits seemed to be lifted. She popped out of the truck, walked up to the gingerbread, wraparound porch, and plopped down in an oversized, white rocking chair.

"I could live here," Claire said. "This is such an 'Out of a dream' place." It was obvious to Butch that The Jasmine House had snapped Claire out of her funk. He was glad, because he hated to grovel!

"Why don't we go inside and see if the sheriff really did make reservations for us?" Butch said. "Since I don't see any cars around the place, I doubt there will be an issue of availability of rooms." Butch opened the door for Claire and followed her inside. The house was absolutely charming, and something like Claire might have imagined out of a Charles Dickens story. The first thing that struck her was the fireplace with a beautiful fire licking the logs it was consuming. The fireplace mantle was impressive as well. It must have been ten feet tall, surrounding a marble inlaid firebox that had a brass screen and matching fireplace tools. The mantle was a gleaming white color, with a picture hung on the wall over the fireplace that had to be four feet tall. The first-floor ceiling was at least fourteen feet high, with ceiling fans hung on extended pipes to keep the room cool in the summertime. There were camelback sofas, embroidered wing chairs, and Chippendale furniture placed around the room in strategic areas. The main living room had to have measured over eight hundred square feet, and there was a homey feeling to it all. Claire was in paradise. The living room opened into what was probably once a butler's pantry area, and the check in desk was located there. Butch took the pen lying on the appointment book, signed them both into the bed and breakfast inn, and looked for some form of life to get more information about their rooms and the policies of the inn. He didn't have to wait very long until a tall, pretty lady appeared at the desk to greet them.

"Hello, you two must be Mr. Butch Todd and Ms. Claire Cavendish. I am Charlotte Phillips. We've been expecting you. Your rooms are ready, and we will be serving supper in about an hour. We will come to your rooms and notify your when your presence is expected at the dining room table." Charlotte motioned with the sweep of her lace covered arm to the formal dining room, already set with heirloom dishes, turn-of-the-century paper-thin crystal, and silver flatware.

"I couldn't help but notice that your last name and the sheriff's last name are the same. Are you related? Is he your husband?" Charlotte smiled but quickly corrected Butch's incorrect assumption.

"Oh, no," Charlotte said. "Conrad is a second cousin on my father's side, hence the same last name. We are about as different as sugar is from salt." Claire wanted to ask who sugar was and who salt was, but she thought better of it. "Before you ask, Phillips is my married name. I did marry, and we were together for twenty years before Charles died mysteriously. We still don't know exactly what he did of, and the coroner tried his best to diagnose the cause of death, but it escaped us. He's been gone for three years now."

"I'm so sorry for your loss," Claire said honestly. "We didn't mean to pry."

"It's fine. Everyone knows what happened, and in a small town like Butler nothing is secret or sacred," she said. "However, I was able to keep The Jasmine House and maintain my lifestyle. Charles left me financially secure." That was all that was said. Charlotte finally said, "If you two need anything you can either knock on the Innkeeper's suite door, or you can lift the telephone in your rooms, and they will connect to my cell phone where you can leave a message. Now, I will let you get comfortable and settled. We serve sherry on the piazza in the afternoons, so you are welcome to take a chair there, watch the local townspeople, and wait for dinner. Your choice." Charlotte excused herself, leaving them standing in the butler's pantry area alone. They looked at their room keys and saw that they read Room 104 and Room 106. A quick survey of the house revealed that their rooms were on the second floor of the mansion, and after Butch had returned to the truck for their luggage, they approach the stairs with curiosity.

* * *

Claire and Butch were not disappointed when they opened the tall, solid wooden doors that led into their rooms. They actually had adjoining rooms, with a passage door inset into the wall. The door was open, making the space look even larger than it was. Claire wanted to get the history of this magnificent house, and she was compiling her questions for Charlotte as she hung her clothes in the oversized closet and put her folding items in the antique dressing table's drawers. Butch had decided to just put his overnight bag on a chair. He never utilized closets and dressers when he stayed overnight in a hotel or other places. The only thing he did hang up was his sportscoat and his overcoat. They would show wrinkles if he just threw them down on the bed. Butch was a typical man—nothing formal was necessary to make him feel comfortable or prepare him for a good night's sleep. Claire looked into his room and just shook her head in pity.

"What?" Butch asked.

"You can use the chest of drawers, the closet for your hanging items, and get settled in, Butch."

"I am settled in," he retorted. "I don't plan to be here that long," he said.

"Maybe," Claire said skeptically.

"Maybe? Do you know something that I don't?"

"What I remember is that we told Mayor Hannity that we would aid his friend in any way possible, and I don't think that Sheriff Phillips has a simple problem. Do you?"

"I'm not too sure what I think right now," Butch said. "From the outset, it appears that there is truly a disturbing underground society operating in Butler and Choctaw County, and I doubt we can solve the sheriff's problems in a day, week, or month. Do you differ with my opinion?"

"What I see is that no one has been willing to confront the hatred and percolating evil that has been running asunder in Choctaw County for years—maybe since the end of the Civil War."

"And you think we can fix that situation quickly?"

"I didn't say that. I said that no one has addressed it head-on. If the sheriff knows what's going on and he won't be honest about it, we may be the ones to help him take a proper course of action."

"Pardon me for speaking my mind, but I doubt two outsiders are going to have that kind of impact upon a bad situation that has been going on for 150 or more years. It sounds like these groups who have gone underground to purposely cause derision and discord began around 1865. If thirty years is considered a generation of people, then we are trying to solve the problems of five generations of people angry about what happened to them and their ancestors. That's quite a task, and we are not prepared to do that, Claire." Butch appeared to be recognizing the feat they were trying to achieve, and he knew the task was more than the two of them could solve in a few days. Claire came over to Butch, looked up into his face, and gave him a kiss, just brushing across his lips as if it was an afterthought.

"Butch, I agree with everything you just said. However, while we can't do everything, we can do something. Why don't we change into comfortable clothes, go down to the piazza and get a nice glass of sherry in anticipation of a fine dinner? We can begin making a plan once we have let our thoughts settle a bit." He agreed, gave her a little hug, and went back to his room to change into jeans and a pullover shirt. Claire took a few more minutes to get ready for their time on the piazza, and she came into Butch's room in a nicely fitting pantsuit, hugging all her womanly curves in just the right places. As they walked down the stairs toward the side porch, they smelled dinner being prepared, and it was a wonderful odor. Dinner was announced to be in an hour, so Claire and Butch could enjoy sitting on the piazza, watching the people walking by watching them.

"What do you guess they are thinking, Butch?" Claire asked.

"I'm not really sure, but I would guess it would be that whatever we are doing here is none of our business. This scene would be very similar in Ashburn were we sitting on the front of the Patterson Mansion porch, assuming we were strangers. Small towns don't particularly like outsiders coming into their domains and upsetting the apple carts."

"I guess you're right, but we are here to help."

"We know that, but some of the very people who need helping are too afraid of the dirty laundry that will be revealed if we discover the evil going on behind the scenes in Butler. I see this like a small crack in a dam. Just a trickle of water seeping through the impossibly thick wall of concrete holding back a deluge of water which would flood the town below the dam if the crack became a hole or destroyed the dam altogether. We just need to define where the crack is and work to making it much larger. You know many of the people living in Butler and Choctaw County don't approve of vigilante justice. One never knows if the next target of those angry, self-righteous people is going to be him." Butch took a sip of the sherry, winked at Claire, and raised his glass for a traditional toast."

"What are we toasting, Butch?"

"To our good luck finding the crack!" he said, smiling like a Cheshire cat. They sat in the wicker rocking chairs until Charlotte, adorning a white apron showing evidence of dinner being created, appeared at the front door and welcomed them inside.

"Shall I join you for dinner?" Charlotte asked her guests.

"Sure," Claire said. "After all, this is *your* house! Anyway, I'll bet there is a rich history you can tell us about The Jasmine House."

"Let me get dinner started to the table, and we can go from there. We are having a tomato bisque for starters, homemade cornbread rolls, chicken and dumplings with fresh vegetables as the main course, and homemade pecan pie for dessert. How does that sound?"

"Fantastic," Butch said. "Let's eat!"

"May I help you serve?" Claire asked.

"Oh, no. I'm an old hand at this. I'll just bring the soup, and we can talk a bit while we enjoy the fresh tomatoes from my garden."

"You made the tomato bisque from scratch?" Claire asked. "I thought all tomato bisque came in cans from the grocery store."

"There are a few brands of canned bisque that I might serve, assuming I had no fresh tomatoes in my garden, but thankfully, I have an abundance this year. Traditionally, tomato bisque is served cold. That's the way I have prepared it tonight, but I can warm yours if you prefer it hot."

"No, this will be just fine," Butch reassured her. He took a big spoonful and his smile widened. It was wonderful. "May I ask a personal question?" Charlotte looked skeptical but agreed to answer. "What is keeping you here in Butler? You could be a chef in a famous restaurant in Mobile, Gulf Shores, or New Orleans. Why do you stay here in the boonies with all your talents?" Claire looked at Butch with a grimace. This might be a sensitive area which Charlotte might not want to discuss. However, they were both surprised by her quick response.

"To be totally honest with you, Butch, yours is not the first question I've faced concerning my continued presence in Butler. Since Charles passed a few years ago, I've had several offers for The Jasmine House, and I probably could relocate to a resort area and ply my trade as a chef or innkeeper. However, until I discover why Charles had to die, I'll be right here in Butler." It didn't escape Butch or Claire that Charlotte Phillips had not gotten closure on her husband's death. Did she suspect foul play in his death as well? Butch thought it was very interesting that they might have another person to question about the irregularities in Butler and Choctaw County.

"Charlotte, Claire and I are going to share something with you that we have not made public in regard to our purpose for being in Butler. We are actually working undercover, if you will, for the sheriff's office, hoping to determine who kidnapped Judge Malone and had him murdered. We think that there is a cult society, unseen but not really invisible, operating in Butler and Choctaw County. It appears the cult has its roots in the mistreatment of the Choctaw Indian Nation and the survivors of the Southerners who were either incarcerated or murdered at the hand of the U.S. Government when they conquered the South in the Civil War. That may sound impossible, but somehow, they have bonded and appear to have a common enemy who they can direct their anger at, and that enemy appears to be any organized government authority. For them it doesn't matter if it's city, county, state, or federal authorities—they are all enemies of this invisible cult. Does that sound strange to you?" Butch and Claire watched Charlotte for any reaction to Butch's revelation of facts.

"Charles was an attorney with the Choctaw County district attorney's office. He was honest, kind, but fearless when performing his duties. Everything went well for him initially when he took the job, but one day he received an unsigned note explaining that his office would not pursue a certain individual, with the overtone that Charles's life would be in danger if he continued on the case. Of course, Charles did his job, and he died mysteriously within a week of the conviction of the person in question. While the coroner did an autopsy, nothing was found that indicated that Charles died of anything but natural causes. However, having been married to Charles for twenty years and knowing how generally healthy he was from day-to-day, the fact that he would drop dead at the age of 45 years was hard for me to believe. I still think that there was either something missed in the autopsy, or the coroner was in on the coverup. The action got the attention of the remaining attorneys in the Choctaw County Courthouse office, and no one has been put on trial for anything relating to the mysterious underground society which everyone knows operates in Butler and Choctaw County. I want justice, but I have resigned myself that I may never get it." Charlotte had not teared up, but her countenance had changed, and it was apparent that she believed every word that she spoke.

"How do you go about getting satisfaction?" Claire asked.

"I was hoping for you two to bring something to light that could expose the cult and allow them to be rounded up and prosecuted." They were finished with the tomato bisque, and Charlotte excused herself to bring the main course to the table.

"Wow!" Claire whispered to Butch under her breath. "This may be our way into the shadowy cult world in Choctaw County."

"We can hope," Butch agreed.

Chapter 8

An Ally in Butler

As Charlotte set the steaming plates of wonderful smelling Southern cooking in front of her guests, Butch and Claire had difficulty remembering that their real reason for being in Butler was not to eat the best Southern cooking which they had ever smelled. It was difficult because the dumplings were calling out to Butch and all of his senses to focus on them and not the investigation. Claire's comment brought Butch out of his stupor, and they began to discuss more about Charles and Charlotte's time in Butler.

"How did you and Charles wind up in a small town like Butler? Do either of you have family here or ancestors who drew you back to town?" Claire asked. Claire laughed when she answered.

"No, we neither had relatives nor any reason to come to Butler, other than the offer the judge of Choctaw County made to Charles if he would set up a legal practice in town. I graduated from Ashburn University in 1995, and Charles was attending The Cumberland School of Law on the Samford University campus in the Birmingham area at that time. We met at a party one of my sorority sisters had organized, and I didn't have a date. Several men had been invited to attend from Samford, Birmingham Southern, and other schools nearby. I was twenty years old, and while old enough to vote I was not old enough to drink alcohol legally, so this handsome man brought me a glass of wine and the rest is history. Charles was graduating from Cumberland that spring, and I was a senior at Ashburn University. We had a whirlwind romance, and in just three months were engaged to be married. After a June wedding, we moved to an apartment in Birmingham, Charles became a junior investigator for a criminal attorney, and I stayed home for a while. We wanted to start our family, but, unfortunately, one of us couldn't complete the task, so we were resigned to be a couple who focused on each other. He encouraged me to get out into the business world, but I didn't want to get caught up in the 'rat race,' so I stayed at home and began creating recipes for everything from hor dourves, to full meals using the local fresh vegetables available at the market. I wrote my first cookbook at the tender age of 27, and then my second one when we moved here about ten years ago. The Jasmine House was Charles's idea to get me more involved in things outside of the house." They were now eating the chicken and dumplings, and the food was absolutely wonderful.

"So, you moved here to open The Jasmine House?" Butch asked.

"Oh, no. The Jasmine House was an afterthought," Charlotte said. "The judge for Choctaw County offered Charles an opportunity which he didn't think he could turn down. The job doubled Charles's income, they provided an expense account, and a down payment on a house of our choosing. We decide to purchase The Jasmine House and restore it to its original condition. It was a task, but after two years we were able to move in, set it up as a bed and breakfast inn, and allow me to use the opportunity to prepare the many recipes which I had concocted over the years. That was ten years ago. Everything was fine for the first few years of Charles's work with the county, until he prosecuted a known white supremacist for castrating and murdering another white man. The man was convicted and sentenced to a long prison term in the William C. Holman Correctional Facility at Atmore, Alabama. You may not know this, but the most vile and horrible prisoners are housed there. The convicted man was murdered by his fellow inmates within a week of his incarceration at

Atmore. The white supremacist underground group threatened Charles at that time, and within a month of the convict's death, Charles had died of a mysterious illness. I was sure it had something to do with poison or some other invisible cause, but the coroner didn't find anything to substantiate my claims. I still believe that he was murdered, and I will simply not leave Butler until his murder is solved." Charlotte had begun to choke up as she spoke, so she changed the subject.

"Since Charles was still in his prime, did the sheriff or anyone at the D.A.'s office order an autopsy?"

"No autopsy was performed, and when I asked why they didn't think they should investigate more for a specific cause of death, I was told that Charles died of natural causes, and that was the end of it. I asked a local attorney if I should sue the county and he said it would probably be just a waste of time and money, and it would stigmatize the reputation of The Jasmine House. Not knowing what else to do, I did nothing. Now, as I look back on everything, I should have insisted that an autopsy be performed on Charles's body." Charlotte began to tear up again, and Butch moved on with his questions.

"Who is the coroner of Choctaw County, and what do you know about him?"

"I don't remember her name, but I think she is related to the sheriff. She has an office here, since this is the county seat, but she travels all over Choctaw County. Her office is just off the square down on 4th Street. The building is windowless and cold. It looks like a great place for a morgue. From what I understand, the hospital stores most of the bodies in the basement in a cold storage locker until the coroner can get to them, according to one of my guests who frequents The Jasmine House." Claire wrote down what Charlotte had said about the coroner, reminding herself to get the coroner's name from Tallulah at the courthouse. It was apparent that Charlotte was still grieving for her lost husband, so Butch and Claire moved on to more pleasant topics for the remaining part of dinner. After they were full, Charlotte suggested that they all take a moment and enjoy a glass of sherry on the wraparound porch of the old Victorian mansion. It sounded like a good idea to Claire and Butch, so they all ventured out on the porch, sat in oversized rocking chairs, and watched the world go by in downtown Butler, Alabama. They all sat quietly for thirty minutes, letting the wonderful food which Charlotte had lovingly prepared, settle in their systems. Butch looked at his watch and it was now 8:00 PM. Much earlier than his normal time to turn in for the night, but he thought it might be good to get a great night's sleep before tackling the sheriff and the white supremacists in the morning. He was going to get to the bottom of the origin of the cult that seemed to be undermining the good people of Choctaw County, and the sooner the better. Butch made his excuses for himself and Claire, and they went off to their respective bedrooms. To say that Charlotte was a well-informed and intuitive innkeeper would be an understatement. The rooms which Butch and Claire had been assigned had a connecting door. They made good use of this convenience, and they felt as comfortable in The Jasmine House as they had ever felt in their own rented hovel in Ashburn. While they retired early that evening after the wonderful meal and the enlightenment which Charlotte was able to relate about her own personal experience with the white supremacists and her personal loss of a husband, they didn't go to sleep immediately. Something about the small town, or possibly the events which they had experienced during that day, gave them both the need for a closeness that only sexual intimacy can fulfill. They turned off the lights in Claire's room and went to sleep completely spent after a vigorous session of lovemaking. Butch thought that he could get used to this.

Morning came early in Butler at The Jasmine House, and when Butch and Claire rolled over in her bed, the smell of hot coffee, bacon frying, and homemade biscuits in the oven was the perfect medicine to get them moving and ready for the day. Butch slipped back into his room, they both showered and dressed for the day, and in twenty minutes both detectives were headed toward the dining room for their traditional Southern breakfast. Charlotte didn't disappoint them in her preparations for a big breakfast for them, with pancakes, fresh biscuits, scrambled eggs, sausage, bacon, grits, and hot coffee all laid out on the sideboard just to the left of the formal dining room table. The food had been placed in warmer dishes, so it was still steaming hot, and it all smelled delicious. It was obvious where she intended for them to sit, with two places adorned with silver flatware, crystal glassware, and cloth napkins placed in ceramic napkin rings in the middle of the Blue Willow dishes.

"Isn't this wonderful?" Claire beamed as she took a chair and looked eagerly at the kitchen to get the signal to begin the feast. Just the Charlotte came through the swinging kitchen door with a pot of steaming hot coffee in her hand.

"Ready for some coffee and a Southern breakfast?"

"Absolutely," Butch said. Charlotte poured coffee for both of them, offered them sugar and cream, and told them to take their plates and make themselves at home at the buffet which had been set out perfectly on the sideboard.

"You two are my only residents right now, so help yourselves to as much food as you desire. When you are finished, I will tidy up and get thing ready for dinner. I'm assuming you will be out for the lunch hour, so I had not planned to prepare lunch for you today."

"Thank you so much," Claire said. "We were a little concerned about where we would get a good mean in Butler, and I guess that question has been answered!" Charlotte thanked Claire for the compliment, and then Charlotte disappeared back into the kitchen and let them have the dining room area to eat and talk.

"Isn't she lovely?" Claire said in a whisper to Butch.

"She is. I would marry her if I didn't already have a girlfriend!" he said and smiled at Claire.

"Oh, is that so?" she flirted back at him. "What if your girlfriend can't cook as well as Charlotte? Wouldn't that concern you?"

"Cooking is only one thing that a marriage partner should be able to do well. My girlfriend can do multiple things well, if you get my drift." They both laughed at his comment, took their plates to the sideboard, and filled them to overflowing with the scrumptious food Charlotte had prepared for them.

"Is the sheriff's office paying for all of this luxury?" Claire asked.

"I don't know for sure, but no one's said anything about needing a credit card or cash deposit. Let's just eat and enjoy!" They both sat back down at their respective places at the table and gorged themselves on the best breakfast that they had had since they had left Ashburn on their way to Gulf Shores. It was obvious to both of them that their rest and recreation trip would have to be rescheduled. They finished breakfast, waddled back to their rooms, and were tempted to crawl back into bed and take a nap, but Charlotte had slipped into their rooms while they were eating breakfast and remade their beds, freshened up their bathroom, and emptied their trash cans.

"Now that is one efficient woman," Claire said. "Are you sure you don't want to propose marriage to her?"

"I'm sure. She's not my type."

"Oh, great cook, great housekeeper, and stay at home woman to keep your domain in proper functioning order—not your type?"

"You know what I mean. I need the *other* thing as well."

"The *other* thing? Can you be more specific?" she teased.

"Sex. You know. Sex. Should I repeat it?" he said beginning to get flustered. Claire was enjoying herself picking at him, but she thought she'd better back off before he got mad at her efforts to taunt him.

"I know," she said quietly, and she leaned over and gave him a big kiss on the lips. "There will be more of that later," she cooed, and she went into her bathroom and closed the door. Butch went to his own room, brushed his teeth, and lay on his perfectly made bed to wait on Princess Claire to return.

* * *

They had left The Jasmine House at 10:30 AM, fully fed and completely rested from a hardy day of investigating the day before. While they had not really solved anything yet, they did turn over some leaves which could stand revisiting. For one thing, what was going on with the pastor at the Butler Lutheran Church and his congregation? Why was there not an autopsy ordered, much less not demanded, by the sheriff's department and the local district attorney's office on Charles Phillips, and who was really pulling the strings in the small town of Butler, Alabama? Those were just a few questions which occurred to Claire and Butch, and they would generate more as soon as they revisited Tallulah Ashalintubbi at the courthouse this morning. They walked into the courthouse and spotted Tallulah immediately giving instructions to some young man who appeared to be as lost as a soccer ball in high weeds. Claire and Butch waited until Tallulah had freed the boy from her instructions, and then they approached her with big smiles.

"Good morning, Tallulah," Claire said with a radiant grin. "Do you remember us?"

"Of course, I do, dear. How may I be of assistance to you today?"

"Butch and I would like to come back when you are on your break and take you across the street for some coffee and apple pie," Claire tempted the elderly lady with sweets and coffee.

"I'm a volunteer, Claire. I can go on break any time I am a mind to do so," she said with a little scoff. "I could use a cup of black coffee and a piece of Lulu's pie right now. Are you going to try and pick my brain again?" she laughed.

"Absolutely," Claire joined her in a chuckle. "There's no one's brain in Butler, Alabama, who I'd rather know what's going on in their head than yours!" All three of them chuckled, Tallulah put her "gone for the moment" sign up at her information station, and they walked together out the front door of the courthouse and across the street to

Lulu's Diner. Claire and Butch had eaten there earlier in the week, and the food was magnificent for a small-town establishment. As they approached the diner, Lulu caught sight of her old friend Tallulah and her new friends Butch and Claire. She asked them if they wanted to sit outside on the sidewalk or inside in a booth.

"I vote for inside," Tallulah said. "We may discuss someone walking by us on the sidewalk and I don't want to offend anyone."

"Inside it is," Claire said to Lulu. "In fact, how about one of those booths towards the back of the diner. May we sit there?"

"You are the customer, honey. You can sit at any unoccupied table in the joint," and Lulu laughed as she walked away.

"Tallulah, have you known Lulu very long?" Butch asked.

"About fifty years. She and her husband opened up that diner twenty or so years ago, and I've been eating there all that time. It's one of the best places to eat in Butler."

"Butch and I ate there earlier this week, and we had a great meal. I'm curious who you think serves a better meal in Butler than Lulu?" Claire teased. Tallulah smiled and revealed just how small Butler, Alabama, was as far as information getting around.

"You know the answer to that question before I even attempt an answer."

"We do?" Claire asked. "Who might that be?"

"Charlotte Phillips, of course. You two are staying there, aren't you?" Tallulah gave them one of her knowing smiles, and the conversation morphed into a more important subject than cooking.

"How long have you known Charlotte Phillips"

"Let me think a minute. She and her lovely husband Charles moved to Butler about ten years ago when he took the job as district attorney for Choctaw County. They had no children, and Charlotte told me that she had always wanted to write cookbooks and prepare fancy feasts for people, so I suggested that they purchase the old mansion which had been pretty much abandoned for twenty years, fix it up as a bed and breakfast inn, and she could try out her recipes on her guests. They took me seriously, and the county helped them acquire the property. It took a long time, maybe more than a year, for them to get it updated and ready to open for business. Charles was a handsome, bright young attorney, and I have no idea why he would want to relocate his pretty and talented young wife to a town like Butler, so I never asked them why they decided to move here. I think the county judge offered Charles a good salary and some other benefits, like helping them acquire the old house, so they became residents. Did Charlotte tell you about him dying mysteriously?"

"She did, and that there wasn't an autopsy performed. He was pretty young to have died of natural causes, don't you agree?" Claire probed.

"All I know is that he had just successfully put one of those horrible white supremacists in prison for castrating and doing all kinds of terrible things to a white man who had been involved with a Native American girl. I think she was Native American, but she could have been an African American girl. Anyway, there's this 'club,' or so they call themselves, who impose vigilante justice to anyone who does things that their little group of men don't approve of.

I'd say that they are racists, but they are much more. They remind me of the things that Adolph Hitler did to Jews, Gypsies, and homosexuals during WWII. They give me the creeps when I think about them. Anyway, once the white supremacist was convicted and sent to prison things seemed to settle down a bit. However, the man was raped and murdered in prison by some gang members, and the local group of men he had been associated with blamed Charles for his death. They openly threatened his life, but there was never any proof of foul play in the cause of his death, according to the coroner."

"Does Choctaw County still have the same coroner who was practicing back when Charles died?"

"Yes, I think he's still the coroner. His name is Dr. Julius Applecorn. I think he's a personal friend of the county sheriff, and he always campaigns with him every time both of them are up for reelection. I think he's a little odd, but I just thought all coroners were that way."

"Do you know where his office is located?"

"He really doesn't have an office, per se, but he operates the morgue out of the basement in the Butler Hospital just on the outskirts of town. It's easy to find. If you take Highway 84 West, you'll see it just outside of the city limits. The hospital administration wanted to build their facility in downtown Butler, but they got crossed up with the sheriff and the county judge, and no one would sell or lease them enough property in town for their building and parking lot. As I recall, there was a big fuss about it, the story made the newspapers, and the controversy eventually just went away. But the sheriff and the judge got their way, and now people have to drive out of town for medical care. It's outrageous, if you ask me," Tallulah scoffed.

"How long has Judge Doran been the circuit judge for the county?" Butch asked.

"Hmmn, let me think," Tallulah said. "I guess for at least twenty or more years. The sheriff has held his position at least that long, and so has the coroner. Folks in these parts don't put strangers into office just because they promise things that the people don't have and would like to get. However, it wouldn't surprise me if the judge, the sheriff, and the coroner were all members of that club that the white supremacist belonged to before he was convicted. Local people have heard the rumors of that club, as well as some other cult operating in the far reaches of the county, but no one seems to want to do anything about exposing them for what they are. People are afraid, especially after what happened to Charles Phillips." Lulu brought coffee all around and slices of apple and cherry pie.

"If I stay in this town too long, I won't fit into my clothes," Claire moaned.

"You're as skinny as a rail, child. You need to eat more and put some meat on those bones. But I guess Romeo here wouldn't like you too plump. Right?" Claire blushed and Butch, aka Romeo, just chuckled. Tallulah was a hoot. "I remember when I was a girl, I worried about my butt getting too big, my thighs and my stomach as well, but when you get to be my age those things don't matter too much." Tallulah let out a big laugh and took a big gulp of her coffee.

"You look lovely to me, Tallulah," Claire reassured her and patted her hand fondly. "Please tell us more about Charles and Charlotte when he died. Charlotte said that he died of mysterious causes, but you said the coroner said it was of natural causes. What was mysterious about his death?"

"The man was in his prime, maybe forty years old, at most. People don't die of natural causes without there being some reason for that happening. I had a chance to talk to Charlotte at the funeral and I asked her if he had cardiovascular disease, or other life-threatening illnesses, in his family line, and Charlotte said she didn't think so. And, assuming that was his medical history, why didn't the attorney general or the sheriff demand or order an autopsy? Didn't that seem strange to you?"

"Honey, many things seem strange to an old Native American woman, but there's little I can do about my thoughts or impressions. I'm not afraid of someone poisoning me or anything like that, because I've lived a long and happy life, but what is going to change? Nothing. I'm telling you some of those local rednecks and my fellow Choctaw relatives are reliving the Civil War over and over, like it is going to change the eventual outcome. They are delusional, and I don't want to be a part of that nonsense at my age."

"You mentioned that you weren't afraid of being poisoned," Butch said. "What did you mean by that?"

"It's no secret around Butler that many people thought that there was foul play in Charles Phillips' death, but no one has enough power to influence the sheriff or the coroner to do anything about investigating any other cause of death than natural causes." Butch raised eyebrows at Claire, acknowledging their mutual concern that the problem might be far reaching, and even further than Sam Hannity had heard from his friend, Conrad Phillips.

"You seem to have your finger on the pulse of what is going on in Butler and Choctaw County, Tallulah. How should we go about finding out more about the possible invisible cult operating in Choctaw County?" Butch asked.

Tallulah thought for a moment without speaking. She finally said, "You're going to need a pow wow." Butch snickered when Tallulah suggested the pow wow, but Tallulah was very serious.

"Butch, a pow wow is simply a meeting of a number of a tribal of people, who dance, sing, and communicate by telling stories about their family's past experiences. Pow wows are open to the public, and people from every background are welcomed to attend the celebration of a pow wow. If there is any information about this so-called cult made up of Native Americans and other people, a pow wow might reveal that fact."

"But we're not Native Americans, Tallulah. We would feel out of place, even if they allowed us to attend."

"You don't have to be Native American to attend a pow wow. You simply have to follow the etiquette of the tribe sponsoring the pow wow. I can help you with that because it is the culture of the Choctaw Indians, of which I am one! Have you ever been to a real pow wow? I don't mean one like you see in Cherokee, North Carolina, or other places that put on a show for a paying audience?"

"No, I can actually swear that I have never been to a real pow wow. Have you Claire?" She shook her head no.

"It sounds like a great time for all," Claire picked up the ball and charge forward with the idea that they should go to one as soon as possible. "How would we get invited to something like that, and do you have connections?" Tallulah smiled broadly, indicating that she had already been planning on getting a pow wow set up for her new friends.

"When do they have these pow wows? Time is of the essence for us in this case, and I'm not sure we have enough time to wait for something so elaborate to be set up and then performed," Butch said.

"You leave it to me," Tallulah said. "I'll have you at a pow wow in a matter of days. I'll also give you the 'dos' and 'don'ts' for the event. The last thing you'll want to do is offend your hosts by disrespecting their customs. When I get back to the courthouse, I'll get right on it. Make sure I have your telephone numbers so I can let you know the time and place for the big event. Isn't this exciting?" Tallulah giggled like a little girl. Claire took out a business card, wrote both hers and Butch's telephone numbers on the back and encouraged Tallulah to call them as soon as she could make things happen.

"Is there a financial charge for the gathering? We'd be happy to contribute if it's necessary or customary for the guests to do so," Claire asked.

"Oh, no," Tallulah said. "Even offering to pay for the pow wow would be considered a slap in the face of the chief of the local tribe. Just count on me getting things set up, and all you two need to do is show up and display respect for the tribal dances and other things that will take place. Once the dancing, singing, and eating is concluded, the chief will invite you and any other guests present at the pow wow to join him in his tent to smoke the peace pipe."

"Neither of us smoke," Claire said. "Will that be a problem?"

"Just take a mouthful of smoke and blow it out. It's part of the ceremony, and you need to be prepared to participate. The chief will allow you, Claire, to join the smoking of the peace pipe ceremony, but Butch will be the one required to share tobacco with the chief. Can you handle that Butch?" Tallulah asked.

"We'll make it work, Tallulah. Thank you for setting this up for us."

"I can't tell you if the chief will have any words of wisdom for you, but if there are any Choctaw Nation members taking part in a cult organization, the chief will know."

"What's his name?" Claire asked.

"The chief's name is Laughing Bear," Tallulah said. "Do you know how the true Native Americans name their children when they are born?" Both Claire and Butch said that they did not. "Naming a child is very important, and naming a male child is even more important than naming a female. Often a newborn child will go nameless for weeks or months before the chief determines what that baby's name will be."

"The mother or father don't name their own baby?" Claire asked in unbelief. "They don't have any input?"

"No, Claire. Many Native Americans believe that the spirit in a child may be from old and may be reborn into the young child. In other words, a person can be born over and over again and possess the life of a newborn child."

"Like reincarnation?" Butch asked.

"Sort of, but not really. The chief will be inspired to name a newborn when the 'Spirit' moves him. For instance, Laughing Bear as named by the chief of his tribe months after he was born, and when the chief was hunting wild game. He came upon a huge black bear that appeared to be laughing at him and his hunting party. Laughing Bear's chief knew in his own spirit that that would be the young child's name."

"Fascinating," Claire said. "I'm guessing that only happens in tribes where they have stayed true to their other beliefs. Am I correct?"

"I would say less than ten percent of Native Americans follow the old traditions. In fact, you might think that my name Tallulah is a modern-day name, but you would be incorrect. The name Tallulah means 'leaping water' in the Native American language."

"So, you were named by a chief?" Claire asked in amazement.

"Not really," Tallulah confessed. "It would be a lie to tell you that, because my mother picked it out long before I was born. She would have named her male child Inola, meaning black fox, but instead she had me. That was in the early 1920s, so it wouldn't have been unusual for her to have permitted the chief to name me. However, she wasn't a big fan of the tribe style of living, so I was reared more like a Caucasian child than a Native American. I did study my people and their origin and customs when I was old enough to strike out on my own. My last name, Ashalintubbi, was my father's sir name, and it means 'You are a leader.' I guess I could have changed my name over the years to fit in better in my Caucasian surroundings, but I actually took pride in my name and heritage. Believe it or not, I met and married a local railroad worker named John Smith. Can you believe it? There was no way I was going to give up my special identity to become Mrs. Smith," she laughed. "I kept my last name, which was very unusual in the 1940s, and John and I stayed married ten years before I caught him stepping out on me. Fortunately, he gave me no children, so I didn't have to consider them before I kicked his butt out of the house. I've been single since then. I've had my chances at love, but I prefer going it alone. The only person I have to please is me!" Claire and

Butch couldn't help but laugh at this octogenarian and her life stories. If either of them had been a writer, Tallulah Ashalintubbi would have been great subject matter for a novel.

"Let's get back to the courthouse, you two get busy with your investigation, and I'll set up the pow wow and then call you with the details. How does that sound?"

"Perfect," Claire said. "We appreciate your help in this matter. People are so clannish in Butler and Choctaw County, so it's nice finding someone willing to confide in us."

"You're most welcome," Tallulah said as they left Lulu's. They had taken the table out of service for more than an hour, so Butch left a $20 tip out of courtesy. Lulu saw it, smiled at Butch, and tucked the bill into her blouse.

Chapter 9

Testing the Water

According to Webster's Dictionary, the meaning of testing the water *is used to describe someone who is exploring the feasibility of becoming a candidate for political office. It can also be used more generally as an idiom meaning to try to gauge the success of something by trying it out a little bit.*

How does one gauge the probability that the local townsfolk will be upset if all their dirty laundry is aired for the world to see? Most people keep secrets because they don't want their activity which they are hiding from the public to meet the light of day. Claire and Butch were encouraged that their session at Lulu's with Tallulah was a positive way to get to know more about the secret culture of the Choctaw Nation. Of course, discovering the evil in a community was one thing, but deciding how to deal with it was quite another. Butch was willing to accept the little things first, betting on the bigger things to come down the road. Tallulah was such a breath of fresh air for the city of Butler, and if she could put them in touch with the chief who knew everything going on behind the scenes, their job would be much easier. Butch spoke to Claire about the elephant in the room.

"You know that we still have to call Mayor Hannity and explain to him about the things that are not how Sheriff Phillips described them. I am beginning to believe that the sheriff may be part of the problem, and not part of the solution. Thoughts?"

"Yeah, I've been thinking the same. From what he's said in the past, the sheriff is a close ally, and the mayor may not believe us."

"We will tell him the truth, and that's all we can do. However, one must ask how something like a cult can exist in modern-day society without the police, judicial system, and government agencies knowing or caring. I can tell you that things don't add up for me. Shall you call him, or do you think I should make the call?"

"You're the senior officer," Claire said. This was one of the first times she could appreciate that Butch, the Chief of Police, had drawn the short straw. Butch agreed and dialed the Ashburn City Hall. Sally Lancaster, the mayor's secretary picked up and told Butch to hold for the mayor. In a matter of seconds, Mayor Sam Hannity was speaking to Butch.

"I was wondering when I would hear from you or Claire. How are things going in Butler?"

"Very interesting, Mayor. Do you want the short version or the long one?" Butch's answer seemed ominous to the mayor, but he let it slide.

"I guess the short version will do for now. Have you and Claire been able to help him at all with his situation?"

"That's what we need to speak to you about, Mayor. I have you on speaker so Claire can listen and join in the discussion." The mayor and Claire exchanged greetings, and Butch continued with his report. "When we came to Butler, we anticipated discovering some form of right-wing, anti-government group of people operating in the shadows of the local society. I'm afraid it's much more than that, assuming that what we have heard from some of the locals is accurate."

"How credible are your sources?"

"Very credible. I'll spare you the details right now, but there is a possibility that there have been conspiracies that include the circuit judge, the coroner, and the sheriff's department. We can't prove anything yet, but one of our better sources is helping us get to know one of the local Choctaw Indian chiefs by attending a pow wow soon. Supposedly, once we go through that experience with him, he will tell us more about any Choctaw Nation people involved in any kind of cult operating in secret in the county. We anticipate that happening any day now."

"A pow wow? Really? You're not just blowing smoke up my pants leg, are you," the mayor laughed.

"Absolutely not, Mayor," Claire said. "We have befriended a very lovely elderly lady by the name of Tallulah Ashalintubbi, a Native American lady who has worked in the Choctaw County Courthouse for many years as a voluntary greeter. If it were not for her, we wouldn't know much more than we did the first day we drove into town. She has put us in touch with a bed and breakfast owner who believes that her attorney husband was possibly poisoned by some white supremacists who belong to a cult. That cult is unusual in that it may consist of both Native Americans who are upset with the government for running them off their ancestral land, as well as white supremacists belonging to an order of the KKK, who never accepted the federal takeover of the South by carpetbaggers after the Civil War. Supposedly, we may get to the root of this group's existence after the pow wow."

"While I must admit that the idea of a pow wow in modern-day Alabama is a bit of a stretch to take in, I am all ears on how you intend to make it work for you. You really believe that Sheriff Phillips is complicit in whatever illegal is going on in Choctaw County? Why would he ask for my help if he had any thoughts that he might be exposed in the investigation? Does that make sense to either of you?" Neither detective spoke for a moment while Butch formulated his best answer to the mayor's question.

"It could be that he possibly thought that we wouldn't discover much, and then he could claim that he tried to find out what was going on in his county if the truth ever came out. And, as you well know Mayor, the truth *always* eventually comes out. I know it doesn't really all add up, but our source swears that the sheriff has known for years that a cult has been causing a lot of pain to the locals over the years. He simply turns his glance away from any signs which might lead him to the truth."

"That's a pretty hard thing to say, Butch. Do you really think he would not uphold the law just to stay on the good side of some radical county residents? After all, he is law and order."

"Mayor, I didn't even want to tell you about our concerns until we had hard proof of what is happening in Choctaw County. However, you asked me for the truth and I'm giving it to you as I only know how. I am being straightforward and honest with you. Maybe Claire can shed more light on what's going on than I can, but the suspicions are highly indicative of someone in a place of influence permitting these cult meetings to continue to operate outside of the law."

"What do you think, Claire. Are you also in agreement with Butch that my friend may be complicit in something illegal happening in Choctaw County?"

"We should know a lot more in another day or two. We are staying at a bed and breakfast inn where the surviving owner believes that her husband was targeted and permitted to be murdered by these cultists, and she may be able to help us expose the facts. She doesn't appear to be afraid of confronting the people whom she thinks targeted her husband for death, but who knows how she will hold up under more pressure. I think we should ride this investigation out until after we have spoken with Chief Laughing Bear, attending their pow wow, and then draw our own conclusions about how much a threat to the general public or the security of the United States of America these radical cultists present."

"As crazy as it sounds right now, you're probably correct in following up on your planned pow wow. If anyone had told me then I was running for mayor that my Chief of Police and Chief of Detectives would be attending a pow wow to gain critical information in a possible murder case, I would have laughed in their faces. It just goes to show that one should never say never!" Claire and Butch could picture the major's face as he hung up the phone and let them get back to their investigation.

"That didn't go so badly," Claire tried to mollify Butch.

"It absolutely did. We crashed and burned!" Butch said.

* * *

Butch and Claire had gone back to the Lutheran Church to see if Pastor Ronald Smith could shed any additional light on the subject of the cults which they knew he had personal knowledge of in his community, but the pastor was uncooperative, saying that there was a sanctity in the covenant a pastor takes with his flock when vowing not to disclose personal information to anyone unauthorized by the one sharing news, even if it meant the pastor could be held in contempt by the police department or the judicial court system. Right or wrong, Pastor Smith was going to keep his vows, and nothing Claire or Butch could say would loosen his lips. Disappointed once more in the pastor, Butch and Claire went back to the diner and spoke to Lulu. It was 3:00 PM and she was just closing up for the afternoon.

"How may I help you this time?" Lulu asked. "I can tell you this much. If Tallulah Ashalintubbi couldn't answer your questions, you'll be wasting both my time and yours trying to get better information from me," Lulu said with a chuckle. "That woman knows everything that goes on in Butler and in Choctaw County. She's your best source for gossip and the real truth going on behind closed doors."

"We have been able to learn a lot about Butler from Tallulah and some other folks in Butler, but we had a few specific questions for you as well," Butch said.
"Do you mind helping us out?"

"While I think it will be a waste of your time, I'll be glad to tell you what I know. I see just about everyone in Butler at least once or twice a week, either in here having a meal, or walking by discussing their private business on the sidewalk. While I'm not a gossip, I do hear things. What would you like to know where you think I can enlighten you?" Lulu motioned them to a table which had been bussed and cleaned for the next patron. As they sat, Lulu picked up a fresh pot of coffee and three cups. She sat the cups in front of them and poured the fresh coffee which was steaming. The aroma was almost enough to wake them up from an afternoon of dreary news and their conversation with Mayor Hannity.

"Let me start by telling you that no one confides in me or my waitresses with gossip, because I don't approve of people telling stories behind their neighbors' backs, and I've made that known to my patrons and wait staff. However, my position on gossip being spread in my diner doesn't always override the juiciest stories spread by the most prominent gossips. I have heard in the past that some people have been threatened by some white guys and Native Americans to not mix together socially or sexually. There are also rumors of men being castrated or otherwise disciplined by these right-wing nuts for showing too much attention to women of another race. They never seem to attack the women, but by making examples of the men, they accomplish their goals of keeping each race pure and undefiled, according to their warped beliefs. Personally, I don't care what color you skin is, your race or your country of origin. Black folks' money spends just as well as Native American's money, and white folks' money. However, when anyone begins to judge other people based upon their own personal beliefs, that's where I draw the line."

"Have you or your staff been threatened in the past by any KKK member or radical Native American person because you have served someone whom they don't approve of?" Butch asked.

"Not to my knowledge, but I really try to ignore as much of that kind of thing as I can. It's not good for business."

"No one has threatened to burn your restaurant down or cause any bodily harm to you or your people in the past?" Claire asked.

"Not really. There are so few places in town to get a good meal, and the town might tolerate biased, racist, angry people under certain circumstances. But if those

radicals tried to burn down one or two of the few eating establishments in town, there would be riot like you have never seen!" Lulu laughed. "I mind my own business and most everyone else minds theirs. That's the way to coexist in a small town," she said. "Now, if you don't have any other specific questions for me, I need to finish cleaning up and get this placed closed. I open again at 5:00 AM in the morning, so I have to get here by 4:00 AM and start the biscuits and other bakery items so we can begin serving at 5 AM sharp." Lulu stood, wiped her hands on her apron, and offered a friendly handshake to her patrons.
"Hopefully, I'll see you tomorrow for one of your meals. I heard that you two are staying at The Jasmine Inn, and I'm hard pressed to deliver as good a meal as Charlotte Phillips can in her fancy B&B, but I try." Condescension was a nice touch for Lulu, as she was probably the next best cook in town, after Charlotte Phillips.

"We will look forward to seeing you again, Lulu," Claire said, taking her hand and giving it a good squeeze. Claire and Butch walked out of Lulu's Diner not much wiser than they had been before they had entered.

PART II: Exposing the Guilty

Chapter 10

Narrowing the Suspects List

"What we really need to do is to narrow the suspects down to a manageable number so we can check out each of their movements in and around the time Dr. Charles Phillips died. I'm reluctant to say that he was murdered, but it's looking more every day like that's what happened. Whether or not that's the case, I think we need to assume that Dr. Phillips was murdered, and someone in the invisible cult was the perpetrator of the evil deed," Butch said.

"It makes sense to me. The cult was punishing Dr. Phillips because one of their own was convicted, sent to prison, and murdered there by an inmate. Whether or not there is a connection between the murdered convict and the cult is a moot point. The cult held Charles guilty of placing one of their people in harm's way, even though the trial and the verdict were righteous."

"We may never be able to prove that assumption, but we really don't have to do so. What we need is for the chief of the tribe to tell us all he knows about his people's possible involvement in the cult. We can take it from there."

"Are we being too ambitious? We don't need an uprising that will swell into a race war between the cult members and the townsfolk."

"What I've discovered over the years is that bullies and racists are basically cowards at heart. They do what they do because they feel inferior to their peers, and they want to be accepted just like everyone else. What we need to do is define who is the head of the snake for this cult, and then we cut off the head and the snake crawls away and dies," Butch said.

"If you are right, and we can find out who is the catalyst of the invisible cult operating in the county, I will get my sword ready to do the cutting!"

"What we don't want to do is to show our hand and give the cult members time to bond against us. Most of the members are probably normal law-abiding residents of the county under ordinary circumstances. Charismatic leaders are known for whipping their followers into a rage and getting them to do things they ordinarily wouldn't think of doing. The first thing we need to do is create a list of people we can trust and who wouldn't give us up to our target, even if they were under duress. We don't need a lot of people, but just enough to help us bring these cowards to justice."

"My list would start with Charlotte Phillips, Lulu Smith, Tallulah Ashalintubbi, and possibly Pastor Smith," Claire said. Butch reacted negatively to the pastor being included as an ally.

"You would include Ronald Smith, after all the dodging he has done with us so far? Explain your logic, because I'm sure you have considered how little he has helped us."

"What do we know about Ronald Smith, objectively speaking?"

"He would take a secret to his grave before he gave up the source of his information, and he doesn't seem to fear punishment for his moral stance. Did that sum him up pretty well?"

"Perfectly! That's why we include him in our list of trusted local informants. He gave us Leroy and Ruby

Smithson's name and identified them as being part of the invisible cult. He's been helpful, but not eagerly coming forth with information we could use. However, I think he would protect our identities just as much as he protected his parishioners who he knew were doing wrong. Doesn't that speak to his good character?"

"What we need to do now is find Leroy and Ruby Smithson and squeeze them for information."

"If he is a trusted member of that invisible empire, what are the odds that he will spill his guts to a couple of strangers like us?"

"Because, Claire, we are not only strangers, but we're also *sneaky* strangers!'

"And how is that going to help us with the Smithson's? You are expecting them to just roll over and tell us what we need to know to smash their little cult into small pieces all over Choctaw County?"

"I'll bet those fine local folks have kids, and maybe grandkids. How would they like to not be able to see them ever again, or at least until the children get to be adults and can petition the court to see their parents? I don't doubt Leroy is probably a good old boy who would go to the ends of the earth to serve his cult leader, that is, until the effects of not cooperating with the authorities hit close to home. Then he might have a change of heart."

"That sounds a lot like blackmail to me, Butch. Is that what I'm hearing?" Claire asked. Would this man whom she really liked and respected stoop to blackmailing a father and mother and threaten to keep them from their kids unless they cooperated?

"Don't think of it as blackmail, Claire. Think of it as choices one makes as they walk through the journey of life!" Butch tried to wax poetic. It failed to impress Claire.

"How would you phrase things to get them to give up their information without truly extorting them with their kids?"

"I would tell a third-party story about a family that got mixed up in some bad stuff and refused the help the local authorities sort things out, and the family was split up for good with the parents and the children having to go their separate ways—the parents to jail and the kids to foster homes. That's informational, not a threat."

"But you know for a fact that such a thing could happen to the Smithson's if they fail to cooperate. Right?"

"I guess, but that's their decision to make. If they are involved in illegal activities, maybe giving the kids to DFCS (the Department of Family and Children Services) is best for the kids. How can I judge?" Butch tried to look innocent of malice, but Claire knew better.

"You're saying that they have to choose between keeping their secrets and keeping their family intact."

"The law is the law, Claire. We simply try to do the best job we can within the broad interpretation of that law. We give the Smithson's the opportunity to purge themselves of guilt and walk free."

"But would they walk free if you bring them up on charges?"

"Who said we would bring them up on charges? We may simply *imply* that those are their choices and see how far it gets us to our goals."

"What if they don't take the bait? You're left hanging out on a limb, looking stupid and like a liar."

"Claire, we all take chances every day when we step out of our comfortable, safe homes into the world around us. You can do everything correctly and still get hit by a bus and die. It's just life. We don't want to upend the lives of Leroy and Ruby Smithson, but we do want to upset their homeostasis!"

"Their what?"

"Homeostasis, or their way of doing things. As long as they believe that nothing bad is going to happen to them if they don't play along with us, they will be stubborn and unhelpful. We need to be seen by them as their saviors, not their executioners."

"I think I understand, but I'm not sure we can pull it off."

"The first thing we have to do is locate Leroy and Ruby Smithson. The rest we will play by ear."

"I'm guessing that we can't bring the police in on our little search as well. If they are complicit, they will not help, and possibly hinder our goal of finding them."

"Exactly."

"Okay, genius. How do we go about looking for someone who happens to be very good at hiding in plain sight?"

"First, we need to determine if they have kids or not. We need to go to our sources and determine if they have kids, and how many they have. Once we know that, we can use the kids as leverage."

"Are we assuming the Smithson's kids are enrolled in the public schools?"

"I don't think we can assume anything, Claire. We need to ask someone who might know."

"Well, we have defined four people who are probably on our side, so which of the four do we approach; Lulu the café owner, Charlotte the B&B owner, Tallulah the county information specialist, or Pastor Smith the preacher?"

"That's tough. I'm thinking we may need to get help from more than just one of them. Which one would have the most information?"

"Probably the preacher, but if we went to him and just asked for his help, we would probably get nothing. However, if he thinks we already know what we don't know completely, he might spill some information which could help us."

"Tallulah has the ability to check county records, such as birth and death certificates, so she might be the best person with whom to start our quest. Are you ready to take another trip to the courthouse?"

"Absolutely," he said. "I can hardly wait." They got back into their pickup truck and drove to the courthouse, noticed that it was now almost 5:00 PM, the official closing time of the Choctaw County Courthouse, and hurried inside to try and catch Tallulah before she left for the day. She was gathering up her things, and she waved to them as she saw them enter the building.

"Did you two forget something?" Tallulah asked.

"In fact, we did," Claire said in a cheery voice. "There is one question we failed to ask you which is very important to our investigation, and we wanted to ask you before you left for the day."

"What is it?"

"Do you have access to the birth and death certificates files in Choctaw County?" Claire persisted.

"I do. What do you want to know?" Tallulah asked the question as if she had total recall and could remember all the names of those born and who had died in Choctaw County.

"We have developed a person or persons of interest, and we now need to know if they have children. You probably don't remember all the birth certificates you've seen in your tenure as historian, do you?" Claire chucked, giving Tallulah a chance to admit that she didn't have perfect memory recall.

"Well, I remember most of them, because I not only file them in the archives, but I also have to make sure the kids are reported to the public school system and the county tax office. If we didn't do that, some of these kids would grow up completely illiterate!" Tallulah laughed. The county tax office records their births to help with the census taken every ten years. The more people we have on the Choctaw County books, the more money the state of Alabama provides for education, health care, and things like that, especially for the indigent."

"If I asked you how many children Leroy and Ruby Smithson had, what could you tell me." Tallulah thought for a moment and then answered.

"They have three kids, aged five, seven, and nine years old. The youngest and oldest is a boy, and the middle child is a girl. I can't remember all their names, but they are all registered in the Butler Elementary School, and the family is one of the more impoverished ones in the county. They also are on subsistence, food stamps, and monthly food rations. I think the husband, Leroy, may be involved in that secret club or cult you are investigating, but that's just an undocumented rumor. Anything else? I need to get home and feed my cats."

"You have cats?" Claire asked with interest.

"I do. I have seven altogether. Two are inside cats and five are outside cats, but they all expect to eat around 5:30 PM. I must run." She waved goodbye before they could ask her to elaborate on the Smithson's kids, but they had enough information to go back to the pastor for more details. That could wait until tomorrow. It was past 5:00 PM and they were getting hungry. They headed back to The Jasmine House for dinner and a glass of sherry. When they arrived and opened the front door, the smell of spaghetti and meatballs, red tomato sauce, and homemade French bread filled their noses with delicious odors of the things to come. It had been a long day, and they were ready for a good meal and a good night's sleep. They visited with Charlotte, had a wonderful meal, sipped their sherry on the porch, and went to bed early. They planned to speak to Charlotte the next morning about what she knew of Leroy and Ruby Smithson.

* * *

Another night of great sleep for them, but both Butch and Claire were too tired to even think of sex the night before. Butch wondered if he and Claire were becoming an old couple before they even had had a chance to enjoy being a young couple. Claire rolled out of bed first, stretched like a domestic house cat, and went into the bathroom. Butch was right behind her, saw her slip naked into the shower, and he joined her quietly. Before she could protest, he had snuggled up behind her and made himself comfortable in a spooning gesture.

"You are a nasty guy," Claire teased.

"No! I'm a horny guy!" he answered, turned her head towards his, and planed a huge kiss on her mouth. They enjoyed the soap, the warm water, and the oversized towels as they pretended to get ready for the day.

"We will never get to breakfast on time like this," Claire protested.

"Breakfast can be warmed up. I'm already warmed up," he said. They fell back into bed together, and thirty minutes went by as quickly as Butch could ever remember. Finally, exhausted once more, Claire got back up, went into the bathroom, and locked the door. No more hanky-panky for him this morning. They arrived at the breakfast table a few minutes after their normal time, but nothing was said by them or Charlotte, even though Claire was sure Charlotte heard them through the walls of the old house. Their host was as gracious as one would expect a Southern bell to be.

"Did you two sleep well?" Charlotte asked. She didn't indicate that the question was asked "tongue-in-cheek," but Claire felt her skin begin to turn pink, and it wasn't from the hot water she had experienced twenty minutes before.

"We slept just fine," Butch reassured her. "We have a few questions we want to run by you, if that's OK with you."

"I'll be happy to answer any questions that I can, Butch," Charlotte said as she handed them both a plate and indicated that the breakfast buffet was ready once more.

"Are these questions related to that mysterious cult you two are investigating?"

"Yes and no," Butch said. "Yes, there are a couple of people involved whom you may know, and we hope you can enlighten us on anything related to them which you may have heard. But, no, we don't have any specific information about the invisible cult which seems to operate unabated by the local authorities."

"My experience with the local authorities has been anything but positive, but I'll share what I know. I believe the sheriff helped cover up the murder of my husband, and had he had a routine autopsy by the local coroner, I'm convinced they would have found that Charles was poisoned. He didn't die of natural causes. He had just had a complete physical a few months before in Birmingham at the University of Alabama Medical Facility, and he was given a clean bill of health. How then was he capable of dying of natural causes at 45 years old only ninety days later. It just doesn't add up to me." This time Charlotte was not teary or crying, but she was emotionally upset. "I want to nail the S.O.B. who took my husband from me! Will you help me do that?"

"We will do our best to get the coroner's reports analyzed by an outside auditing firm, and we have requested that the governor's office look into possible corruption at the Choctaw County Courthouse. Butch and I will keep you informed as to how that is going as things develop." Charlotte nodded, went back into the kitchen, and brought out some fresh biscuits.

"Better butter these before they get cold. I'm going to lie down for a while. When you're through with breakfast I will clear the table and get the dishes out of your way, in case you want to work at the table this morning."

Charlotte shuffled out of the dining room in a lackluster motion. They had not seen her in a depressed mood like this since they had checked into The Jasmine Inn three days ago. Claire felt compassion for Charlotte, but she figured the best thing she could do for their host was to get enough on the sheriff and coroner to have them removed from office or convicted of crimes against the oath of their offices.

"We'd better get a move on. We never got to talk to Charlotte about the Smithson kids. Let's go by the Lutheran Church and see if we are more successful with Pastor Ronald Smith," Butch said. "I think if we give him the impression that we know more about the overall family than we do, we may get him to open up some and tell us more about how to reach them. He must have an address or an idea of where they live." They arrived at the Lutheran Church and entered the nave. Pastor Smith was straightening the hymnals and picking up the weekly Sunday bulletins strewn around the pews and left by his congregation after their last meeting.

"I see you two are back," Pastor Smith said. He was not unfriendly, but his tone was anything but welcoming. "I've told you all I can about the people of this community, so you're probably wasting your time coming back to hash things all over again."

"Thank you, Pastor. We don't need any information from you about the secret cult operating in Choctaw County. We believe we know all we need to know about them, and this is really just a social call," Claire said. She handed the pastor a cup of fresh coffee and gave him her 1000-watt smile. From his body language, Claire and Butch could see that Pastor Smith had relaxed and no longer appeared on the defensive.

"To what do I owe this pleasant visit?" he asked. "Are you here to gloat?"

"Gloat about what?" Butch asked. "We simply want to help the sheriff and the city and county government control the illegal activities going on that appear to be tearing this community apart. If that's gloating, I must have misunderstood the meaning of the word," Butch said. He and Claire had discussed that they needed to look a little defeated to the pastor, and then maybe he would feel compassion and share more information about the Smithson family. From the look on Pastor Smith's face the ploy seemed to be effective.

"I'm sorry if I came across harsh, but I do have my duties as a pastor to this flock to protect them from all the evil that I can," he said with conviction.

"No one is doubting your sincerity, Pastor Smith. We all want the same thing here," Claire said. By putting all of them on the same side of the issue, they would become allies, not enemies in this fight.

"If there were some other ways to help without betraying my flock, I would help you and the legal authorities, but I just don't know what else I can do." Claire was thinking that this was the perfect setup for their next move.

"Pastor, do the Smithson's kids attend church regularly with their parents? I would think that a five-year-old, a seven-year-old, and a nine-year-old child would need lots of guidance from the Church," Claire laughed. "With the little girl being the middle child, how does that affect the way her brothers treat her?" Now was the time to shut up and let the pastor speak. The question would either be answered with the names of the kids, or Butch and Claire would have to probe deeper.

"Cute kids," Pastor Smith said. "Joey, the youngest, is the one who stays in trouble all the time, and Karen, the little girl, is the one who tries to negotiate between her big brother and her little brother. Terrence, being the oldest, tries to compensate for them being isolated in the woods for most of their lives. But, overall, I'd say they are pretty well-adjusted kids." They hit the jackpot! Without knowing what he was doing, the pastor gave them enough information to make the implied threat of loss of their kids a reality to the Smithson's when Butch and Claire were able to sit them down and talk to them.

"Pastor, we just wanted to stop by and thank you for your help in the past few days. We hope all of this has not upset your congregational gatherings," Claire said. The pastor acknowledged the compliment and thanked them for coming. He let them out of the nave by way of a side door.

"That's half of what we need," Butch said. "Now, we only need to locate the residence of the Smithson family and we will be in business! Any ideas of how we might do that?"

"Sure," Claire said. "We need to visit Tallulah again. We also need to get the coordinates of the pow wow for tonight. I'm looking forward to experiencing Native American culture as it should be, and not as we often see it performed in commercial settings. We should invite Tallulah to go with us to the pow wow, and she can interpret the dancing and other rituals which take place."

"Do you think she would agree to attend with us?" Butch asked.

"Let's invite her and see what she says." They got into Butch's pickup truck, Claire wrote down the names of the three Smithson's kids names, and they headed back to the courthouse. Tallulah appeared to be waiting for them, and she hurriedly put her "Out to Lunch" sign out once more. Moving them towards the outside doors or the courthouse, Tallulah whispered a message to them.

"I have the location of the pow wow for tonight. Would you mind terribly if I tagged along?"

"It's funny you should ask, Tallulah," Claire said. "We were just getting ready to invite you to attend the pow wow with us and interpret the rituals as they are being performed. Would you agree to do that for us?"

"I would love to, Claire. The pow wow is at 8:00 PM, and if you will pick me up in your vehicle, I will direct you to the spot where everything will be happening. First, I need to warn you that you may not take photographs or recordings of the ritual. It is considered rude and inappropriate for an outsider to document the sacred rituals performed at a pow wow. However, the chief will let you know when you can turn on your recorder to document your visit. You must not think of the pow wow as being a social outing, but rather more like a religious service at a church. You should remain calm, solemn, and stoic throughout the process and until the pow wow is ending. At that time, Chief Laughing Bear will accept your questions about his tribe and answer them as honestly as he is able. Do you think you can remember all of that?" Tallulah asked.

"We will try, but we will have you there by our side to advise us if we start to do something that is disrespectful. Right?"

"Yes," Tallulah said. "I will guide you."

Chapter 11

The Pow Wow

With absolutely no disrespect intended, Butch and Claire had to wonder how many people outside of the local tribe of Native Americans ever got to experience a true pow wow as it had been practiced and handed down culturally over hundreds of years in a tribe's history. When Butch and Claire had left the city of Ashburn a few days ago enroute to the white sandy beaches of Gulf Shores, having an opportunity to experience such a revelation would have been far from their minds as potentially available, much less something that they were going to witness and take part in. But here they were getting ready to attend a live pow wow with a genuine Native American woman who represented the tribe they were going to visit. Being invited to such a ceremony by none other than the chief himself, Butch and Claire had no idea what was going to happen at the ceremony. Tallulah asked them if they normally carried weapons, and they admitted that they did. She told them that they would not be welcome at the pow wow if they were armed, so they would need to leave their firearms in the truck until the ceremony had concluded. They agreed and expected that no one else would be armed as well, so it didn't bother them to be helpless and at the mercy of the tribe if something bad happened. The three of them were driving down what appeared to be some old logging road, when Tallulah told them to take a right onto what seemed to be a wide grassy path. They could only drive a short distance before the road ended.

"What do we do here?" Butch asked Tallulah.

"We walk," she said. They walked about a half a mile, and Butch and Claire were impressed that an 80+ year old woman could navigate through the woods so well. It was very dark with no lights of any kind showing in their surroundings, other than a small flashlight Tallulah held in her hand, and then suddenly they came upon a large clearing. The site reminded Butch of a baseball field, with tee pees surrounding the open space in the center rather than dugouts and bleachers. The light and smoke from the small fires in front of each tee pee illuminated the site enough for them to see the men and women in their ceremonial dress. It was surreal to Butch and Claire, because they had only experienced sights like this from watching movies or attending plays. They were escorted to an area covered with deerskins, and they were instructed to sit on the ground and to not speak. Butch and Claire were so surprised at the realistic setting that they wouldn't have known what to think if they had been forced to speak. After sitting down, six men in breechcloths and loin cloths for attire sat down next to them. No one had any head ornamentation other than Chief Laughing Bear, who walked up to them, bowed from the waist in recognition of them being the honored guests of this pow wow. Chief Laughing Bear wore a very ornate headdress of eagle's feathers, colorful beads sewn onto a headband which also sported various other types of feathers of birds of prey. Butch estimated that there must have been twenty or more feathers and hundreds of beads that made up the impressive war bonnet. The chief also had a sheath of leather strapped around the middle of his leather pants which held a tomahawk and a bone-handled knife with a seven-inch blade. All that was missing was a horse and a bow and arrow and Chief Laughing Bear could have been a perfect character for any wild western movie representing the conflict between the Native American race and the white man dating back 150 years. While none of the warriors sitting on their blanket had bows and arrows, they did all have spears with deadly looking pointed heads, appearing to be carved from bone or flint. If one were to close their eyes and let their mind wander, they might imagine that they were in the presence of historic Native Americans who hunted, fished, and defended their tribes with these crude weapons. One of the events at the pow wow was the bow and arrow competition, and Butch was looking forward to seeing just how accurate these warriors were with a bow and arrow.

"Watch the women dance," Tallulah whispered to her new friends. Just then several young women arrayed in the most colorful dresses and shawls began to perform a ritualistic dance, intricate in its motions and repetitive steps, and imitating the movements of large birds of prey. This lasted for ten or more minutes, and the warriors on Butch and Claire's blanket began to move around in sync with the dancers without getting to their feet. It almost appeared to be a dance of sexual provocation, but that may have just been Claire's imagination. All the time the dancers were performing, several young warriors sat behind the chief and played enthusiastically on their tom toms. Unlike modern-day bands with multiple drums, there appeared to be one huge drum and many drummers exercising their skill at the same time on the same tom tom. Along with the dancing and drumming, multiple chants in their native language filled the air like as many firecrackers on the fourth of July. Both Butch and Claire were impressed, and not just because it was loud and showy. There was no doubt in their minds that such a culture should be represented and enjoyed indefinitely. These sovereign people were hustled off their land, cheated out of their birthright, and herded to another state hundreds of miles away from their traditional homeland just to satisfy the lust and desire of their conquering enemies to gain power and wealth. By the end of the pow wow Butch and Claire had a completely different outlook on Native

Americans and their place in the history of Choctaw County. As the dances and chanting began to be phased out, Chief Laughing Bear motioned to Claire and Butch to join him in his tent. They were surprised when they entered that it appeared that the leader of the local tribe of Choctaw Indians actually appeared to be living in the tee pee. It was primitive, with a straw bed, bamboo chest made from local bamboo shoots which were common to the area, and a type of coal-burning stove in the center. A hole in the roof of the tent allowed the smoke and some of the heat to escape through the roof of the tee pee. There were two other small mats for smaller people, and Claire assumed they were for his children. At first, Claire and Butch feared that the chief would not understand them because they didn't speak the language of the Choctaw Nation, but he surprised them with perfectly pronounced English consonants and verbs.

"I understand from Tallulah Ashalintubbi that you have a question or two for me concerning some of the tribe. Please ask your questions," Laughing Bear said.

"We appreciate the invitation to your pow wow, Chief. It was quite amazing and beautiful at the same time. I pray your culture is never erased from this country," Butch said. Claire was surprised that Butch had been so moved by the event, but she could understand his comments.

"Thank you, Mr. Todd. We tell our stories to our children, much like the Hebrews did to their children for thousands of years, and we instill within them the culture of our ancestors. While the land around us has changed over time, our traditions will live on as long as there are two or more Choctaw Indians alive to share that knowledge with the next generation." Butch was amazed at this man's courage and confidence that the modern white man's culture was not going to obliterate the hundreds of years of history of the Choctaw Nation. Butch was glad that he and Claire had made the decision to come to the pow wow.

"Chief," Claire began, "we are trying to uncover an invisible cult which is operating in your area and whose mission appears to be to destroy the culture of the Choctaw Nation and infuse your people with hatred toward the U.S. Government. We understand that the Choctaw Nation was cheated out of their birthright and tricked out of their land but trying to take on the U.S. Government as guerilla fighters is not the answer to regaining respect for your people. What we have been told by the townsfolk of Butler is that some of your Choctaw citizens have formed an alliance with the KKK, a hate-filled organization created to cause havoc in the general population. There are people who have been harmed and possibly killed by this cult, and it has to be stopped and purged out of your land. Otherwise, it will become a cancer and the federal authorities will send armed people to Choctaw County to find and destroy them. If they only destroyed the cult and its people that might be acceptable, but you know how things like that work. Too many innocents get caught up in the struggle and are hurt or killed as well. We want to prevent that from happening." The chief closed his eyes while Butch was speaking and opened them to answer Claire's concerns.

"How can we help you in your cause?" Chief Laughing Bear asked.

"We need a list of any Native Americans whom you think may be involved in such a group, and we need to locate a white man and his family who may be responsible for some of the illegal activities being perpetuated on Butler and Choctaw County. The man and his wife are named Leroy and Ruby Smithson. They live somewhere in the woods in Choctaw County, but we have no idea where that is."

"I cannot surrender any of my fellow Choctaw Nation family members to you. I can try to discourage their involvement with those radical KKK members you mentioned. We are aware of the kinds of things that they do to intimidate their members and others around them. While we appreciate the purity of our race, we do not forbid marriage of our people to any other race of people. That is their concern alone. While there may be a few Choctaw County natives among the cult you mentioned, there could not be many because we teach all of our tribesmen to follow the laws of the land as well as those of the white man. I will give you my oath that I will do what I can to prevent Choctaw natives from joining such a group. As to your second question, I can give you the exact address and an easy way to find the Smithson home. They have brought death and destruction to this land, and they need to be removed." The chief told Butch and Claire where they might find Leroy and Ruby's house, and then he stood, bowed to his guests, and motioned for them to leave his tent.

"The chief is not too subtle," Butch said and laughed as he and Claire walked back to the clearing to retrieve Tallulah. She had been talking with the other women of the tribe while the chief gave Butch and Claire an audience.

"No, he's a man of a few words," Claire agreed. "Let's get Tallulah and get out of here." They motioned to Tallulah to follow them to their truck, they all got into the vehicle, and Butch took off towards town. In a matter of minutes, they were on the asphalt ribbon of highway headed back into Butler. Tallulah spoke first.

"Were you pleased with the pow wow, and did Chief Laughing Bear give you the information you needed?"

"I thought it was divine!" Claire gushed. "I've never been so impressed with a group of people than with those dancers and chanters of the Choctaw Nation. I guess their parents taught them those activities, because I have never seen or heard anything like it in my life."

"The Choctaw tribe today teaches its children all the traditional dances of their ancestors," Tallulah said.

"You mean that there is more than one dance?" Claire asked.

"Oh, yes," Tallulah said. "There's the Bow and Arrow Dance, the Doll Dance, Snake Dance, Buffalo Dance, Grass Dance, and the Devil Dance, just to name a few. All tribes don't perform the same dances, but many of them do similar ones. It's the same with their chants. Also, most of the Native American tribes played Lacrosse, which has survived the test of time. Many academic scholars give the Native American tribes credit for creating an early version of baseball, which they called stick ball, and everyone knows the cultivation of corn and maze was founded in the cultures of the Native Americans."

"It's a shame so much of that culture has been trodden down by European Americans," Claire said.

"Well, that's the nature of the world. When one nation of people conquers another nation, they tend to impose their own cultures and standards on their captives or slaves. Going back to the beginning of time, the Egyptians, Phoenicians, Greeks, and Romans all captured foreign lands and imposed their cultures on their captives. There's nothing new here with the Native Americans. Only in America would anyone even question the eventual fate of the world—the winner makes the rules. The Choctaw Nation will not fade away as long as it has leaders like Chief Laughing Bear to teach and lead the younger generation who come after him."

"Well, I found him totally charming," Claire said.

"You didn't feel threatened while you were on his land and subjected to his rules?"

"Absolutely not. I think the entire Choctaw tribe in this county appear to be the most civilized people I've met."

"Did he tell you how to find your elusive Smithson family?"

"Yes, and as soon as we drop you off, we will check it out."

"Are you sure you don't need my help?"

"Not for that chore, and it might get dicey when we confront them."

"Well, this certainly has been fun for me," Tallulah said with a smile. They were back at the county courthouse, and they asked if they might drive her home. "I only live a couple of blocks off the square, and I like to walk. I'll see you again when I see you," she said, waved a small hand as she got out of the truck, and disappeared into the night.

"You've been quiet tonight, Butch. Are you OK?"

"Yeah, but I'm a little sad. Those people we just witnessed during their ceremony appeared to be some of the most innocent and happy people I have ever witnessed. They were having a blast with their dances, drums, and chants. I'm like you about them losing their birthright. It just doesn't seem fair."

"It's not fair, Butch, but as Tallulah said, it's life. We don't always get to make the situation which we are thrown into, but we can affect how we deal with those situations. I think for the most part the Choctaw Nation has done well to retain its own identity after all the tragedy it's been dealt."

"I can't argue with you there, Claire. But, back to the subject of why we attended the pow wow, what do you think about trying to find the area tonight where the Smithson's live while its fresh on our minds?"

"I say we go back to The Jasmine House, get a good dinner under our belts, rest and recuperate until morning, and then begin our hunt for the Smithson's in earnest. These people would just as soon shoot you at night as they would a stray dog. Let's find the house, stake it out for a while, and then approach them. Anyway, I'm getting hungry for some Charlotte Phillip's cuisine!"

"That's the best idea you've had so far. By the way, did you get the impression that Chief Laughing Bear was going to take care of any Choctaw tribe member involved in the cult for us?"

"That's the impression he gave me, and he seems to be revered by all the subjects we witnessed tonight at the pow wow. Let's give him a chance to get that done, and if we confront Choctaws along the way as we're trying to clear up the invisible cult of Choctaw County, we'll deal with them as necessary. I'd much rather leave that to Laughing Bear, wouldn't you?"

"Absolutely!" They drove to The Jasmine Inn, slipped in quietly to avoid waking their host, but they found her sitting at the dining room table sipping on a glass of sherry.

"Are you two hungry?" Charlotte asked.

"It's too late to ask you to make anything for us. We went to a pow wow with Chief Laughing Bear of the Choctaw tribe, and it was really an experience for which I am glad we had the opportunity to witness," Claire said.

"Did they feed you?"

"Not really, but it's almost ten o'clock, and eating a big meal at this time of the night would probably keep us awake all night," Butch said. Charlotte thought for a moment and then tempted them with a wonderful idea.

"I tell you what I'll do. I have some fresh strawberries and a pound cake that I made earlier in the day. Let's have some coffee and strawberry shortcake with whipped cream. What do you say?"

"That's too much to resist. Are you sure you don't mind fixing it so late? We didn't plan on waking you up, much less having you prepared anything for us this late in the evening," Claire said. Charlotte had already risen from her chair and moved towards the kitchen. In less than five minutes she had a delicious-looking dessert consisting of a one-layer white cake, a mountain of strawberries, and lots of whipped cream smothering it all. As they reached for the cake Charlotte took the coffee pot and poured three cups of coffee. They began to eat the dessert and both Butch and Claire realized how hungry they were.

"Please tell me about your adventure in the woods!" Charlotte said. "I've always wanted to go to a pow wow, but no one ever invited me. I think it's reserved only for those who the tribal chief believes is worthy of including in the ceremony, or so I've been told."

"That makes us feel really special," Butch said. "We were both impressed with the genuineness of the chief and the participants. We didn't know what to expect, and our only other knowledge of such events was related to places like Cherokee, North Carolina, where the Indian dances and chants are focused on entertaining the paying customers. This experience tonight was nothing like that. It was pure, unadulterated ceremony and adoration of their ancestors and tribal customs. We were both blown away.

"It sure sounds nice. Was the chief able to help you discover what you needed to know?"

"He gave us a lead on the man and his family who is a member of the invisible cult, and we hope to look for him tomorrow. We thought about trying tonight, but he might have shot us if we appeared a threat to him, especially in the dark."

"Good for you. Don't go foraging around in the woods around here after dark, Butch. That's truly a great way to get shot, and no one would blame a homeowner after all the mischief that has happened here in the past few years. Tomorrow will be soon enough to find your man." Charlotte offered them more coffee, told them that it was decaffeinated, and everyone enjoyed a warmup. After they were full of cake and coffee, Butch excused themselves, and they went to their bedrooms. Claire was through the joining passage door in minutes, butt naked and ready to jump into bed with Butch.

"Well," Butch said as he took off his pants. "To what do I owe this pleasant surprise?" He turned back the covers and they both launched themselves into the queen-sized four-poster bed, complete with a lace canopy.

"Something about the Native American experience made me feel romantic. You don't mind, do you?"

"Mind? No, I don't mind at all," Butch answered, taking her into his embrace and sliding under the stuffed feather comforter. They went to sleep after their lovemaking and didn't wake again until the sun was peeking through the curtains on the window facing east. Butch looked at the clock and saw that it was only 6:00 AM, so he asked Claire if she wanted to get her shower first or did she want to rest a while until he had finished bathing and dressing. She chose to get up first, so Butch rolled back over an went back to sleep. Just as Butch was getting back to sleep the overhead light came on and Claire announced that it was Butch's turn in the shower. Reluctantly, he rolled out of bed, tramped into the bathroom, and turned on the shower. Both were ready to go to the table for breakfast at 7:00 AM, the regular time that Charlotte put the food on the buffet for them to eat. When they went into the dining room everything smelled wonderful. Pancakes, sausage, bacon, eggs, grits, and homemade biscuits. Charlotte greeted them with her white apron on and handed each of them a cup of steaming black coffee.

"How did you sleep?" Charlotte asked. They knew that she knew that they were only using one of the rooms for sleeping, showering, and for recreational purposes, but there was no reason to discuss those things. Charlotte was being paid by the county to put up two people in separate rooms, and that's what she was invoicing the county for.

"We slept well," Butch said. "That breakfast smells delicious!"

"Help yourselves. That's why I prepared it," Charlotte said as she slipped back into the kitchen for another pot of hot coffee. "Is there any chance you will discover enough evidence to have the sheriff and the coroner investigated?"

"It's really too early to tell," Butch said. "We haven't forgotten our conversation with you about your husband's untimely death, and once we expose any wrongdoing at all, I'm sure we can suggest that your husband's body be exhumed and an autopsy be performed, assuming you still want that to happen."

"I owe it to Charles and to myself to know the truth," Charlotte said.

"Just don't get your hopes up too much until we run these cult people to ground. I suspect that once they discover how much trouble that they are in they will be more comfortable naming their accomplices than just taking all the heat themselves. But first, we must find them and bring them to justice. It may take some time."

"I'm not going anywhere," Charlotte said, and she took another sip of her coffee. Butch and Claire ate entirely too much food, went back to the room and brushed their teeth and performed other grooming chores, and they walked out of The Jasmine Inn at 8:00 AM on the button. Their next stop was somewhere in the woods in the western part of Choctaw County.

Chapter 12

Hiding in Plain Sight

Chief Laughing Bear's instructions to the area where the Smithson's were suspected of living weren't the kind of instructions one would find on a Rand McNally map. He had told them that they needed either a four-wheeler or a good pair of walking boots to reach the place where the Smithson's cabin was located. According to the rumors circulating all over the county, Leroy Smithson took his kids to school, as required by law, in his four-wheel-drive pickup truck. The only time Ruby Smithson was seen in town was when she was spotted in the Piggly Wiggly food store, or at the Lutheran Church on Sunday mornings when all the family worshipped together. Otherwise, she was a ghost in the minds of the people of Butler, because Leroy never permitted her to go anywhere without him to control who she saw and what she had to say about their lifestyle. Their three kids were young, with the oldest being less than ten-years-old, but Ruby looked ten years older than she probably was. Leroy didn't believe in his wife dressing provocatively, using makeup, or having her hair and nails done in town by a beautician. The kids went directly to school and returned home directly after school. They rode a school bus to an area close to their home, then they tromped out through the woods to their primitive house which Leroy and his brother had built for their family twenty years ago. Chief Laughing Bear told Butch and Claire that they should be prepared to defend themselves with firearms if they ventured too close to the Smithson cabin. Laughing Bear had given them several landmarks to go by to know when they were getting close to the area where the cabin was located. It couldn't be seen from the road, but once a person had walked 100 feet into the thickets growing between the highway and the open fields, you could see the house clearly, sitting out in an open pasture with nothing but open land between the house and the crops which were planted nearby. They found the last marker the chief had mentioned, Butch pulled off the road into a clearing, and he and Claire got out of the pickup. Fortunately, they had packed walking boots in their gear when they had decided to take their vacation in Gulf Shores. They had planned to go to a wildlife preserve and walk among the snakes and other wild creatures in the public zoo, but that plan had been jettisoned after Sam Hannity had suggested they look in on his old friend, Sheriff Conrad Phillips. Walking through privet hedges and other thick undergrowth was not what Claire considered pleasant, but they both agreed that it had to be done if they were to get a chance to interview Ruby Smithson alone. Once Leroy went to work at the papermill, he was gone until dinnertime. Both Claire and Butch had taken the safety straps off their sidearms just in case they had calculated incorrectly, and Leroy caught them on his property. As they walk quietly through the woods, Butch would point out to Claire things for her to avoid stepping on, as well as watching for snakes and other unfriendly critters. They had gotten within fifty feet of the cabin when a middle-aged woman came out on the porch with a shotgun in her hands. She called out to them, and Butch answered her back.

"Who is trespassing on my property?" Ruby said, pumping a shotgun shell into the chamber of the weapon she was holding. She was looking around intently, but she hadn't spotted Claire and Butch at that time. Butch took out his white handkerchief, waved it above his head, and slipped out of the thicket and into the clearing.

"My name is Butch Todd, and I am with Claire Cavendish, and we are here to talk to you about your husband and his involvement with some bad people. We need to talk to you, Ms. Smithson, or you have a chance of losing your kids to DFCS, the Department of Family and Children's Services. Will you let us come closer so we can chat together?" She said nothing for a moment and Butch queried her again.

"You can talk where you are," she said. "What do you mean somebody's going to take my kids away from me? That's not right!" Ruby dropped the barrel of the gun, so it was pointing to the ground instead of at Butch and Claire.

"Ruby," Claire used her first name to try to get her to let down her guard, "will you please talk to us? We mean you and your three kids no harm, but you need to talk to us."

"My Leroy will deal with you when he gets home, so go away!"

"Ruby, if we leave here without talking to you, we are going to have to report to the DFCS that your three children are in danger and should be removed from this house and from you and your husband. Is that what you want?" Again, another brief pause before Ruby spoke again.

"We ain't hurting anyone, and no one has the right to come on our land and take my kids away from me. What did we do to make that happen?" Butch and Claire slipped out of the bushes and began making their way toward the small cabin. Once Ruby saw that the woman was young and pretty, and the Butch was handsome and tall, she immediately felt less threatened by their presence.

"Ruby, we know that your husband is involved in the cult that's operating in Choctaw County, and we need to speak to you about what you know about those events."

"What do you want to know?"

"When they meet and where they meet. If we can prevent them from harming anyone else, you and your kids' lives will return to a more normal lifestyle, instead of hiding from people and living in the woods," Butch said. Claire was studying Ruby's face to determine if Butch's words were sinking into her stubborn mind.

"Ruby, there's going to be a federal task force coming to Choctaw County sooner or later, and you don't want to be caught up in that mess. You have a chance to help us determine what happened to Charles Phillips, Judge Malone, and others who have gone missing from Choctaw County and the city of Butler. We can give you protection, and you and the kids can escape this horror," Claire said.

"Why should I get involved? The kids and I haven't done anything wrong. We just have a husband and father who's caught up in all that hate language and the things I hear that they do to those people who don't agree with them." Claire knew this was the best time to get her message across, so she went for it.

"Ruby, do you understand that the Department of Family and Children Services can take your kids away from you, and there's a chance you may never see them again?"

"They can't do that! This is America, and we have rights!" Ruby said, becoming enraged at the thought of someone else taking care of her children. "Can they really do that?"

"Of course, they can do that," Butch said. "It only takes a judge to declare you unfit to take care of your kids, and they will be placed in foster homes."

"Well, Judge Louis Doran won't do that. We have too much on him. He will regret doing anything to help anyone take my kids. I'll tell everything I know about their secret cult, including the involvement of Sheriff Phillips and Judge Doran. They have blood on their hands!" Realizing that she had said too much, Ruby told them that she had said enough, and that she wanted them off her property. She raised the shotgun once more, pointing it at the feet of her visitors.

"Ruby, you really don't want to do this. If your husband decides to make a stand against the law enforcement officers who come to your home to arrest you, you and your children could die in an altercation. Do you really want to put them in that kind of danger?" Claire said, and she purposely stepped closer to Ruby, holding out her hand for the shotgun. Ruby hesitated for a moment, but then she dropped the barrel of the shotgun back to the ground, and she passively surrendered it to Claire.

"You know if I say something against Leroy that he will make me disappear like those other people he helped kill. I'm scared of the government coming after me and my kids, but I'm also scared of my husband. He told me that if I ever crossed him, he would kill me and bury me in the woods where no one would ever find me."

"Don't you think he was probably just trying to scare you to keep you silent?"

"I don't know, but if I help you with your investigation, you will have to hide me and my kids from my husband and his friends."

"We can arrange that, Ruby. We can get the U.S. Marshal Service to put you in Witness Protection where Leroy and the members of his cult cannot locate you to harm you and your kids."

"Would we have to move?"

"Most likely," Claire said. "But they would find a nice safe place for you and the kids so you will not be harmed by Leroy and his friends. You would have to agree to testify against him and the other members of the cult in a court of law, but the Marshals would keep you safe until the trial, and then they would relocate you afterward with a completely new life."

"OK, I'll tell you what I know, but someone will have to pick up my kids from school before Leroy finds out that I have betrayed him and his friends."

"Don't think of it as a betrayal, Ruby. Think that you have help get some very dangerous people off the street and into prison where they won't be able to harm anyone else," Claire said. Ruby chuckled at Claire's statement, and Claire asked her what was so funny.

"Those boys will never go to jail. They will hold up in one of their fortress-like houses and fight to the death with the people who come after them. It will be like that place in Texas where they had the shootout and everyone inside was killed."

"Ruby Ridge?" Butch asked.

"Yeah, that sounds right. Leroy told me that they had enough guns and explosives to hold off a small army if they were ever threatened or attacked by the government." Butch began to show some concern as Ruby told them more about the preparations that they had taken to keep from being arrested in case of a firefight.

"Do you know what kind of weapons they have stockpiled?" Butch asked.

"I'm not totally familiar with those kinds of guns, but Leroy bragged about them having a grenade launcher, some shoulder-fired rockets, and lots of C4, which he said was plastic explosives. They also have hundreds of weapons and thousands of rounds of ammunition hidden in several basements of the homes of their club members. He told me that they could be in a secure, impenetrable fortress in less than an hour's notice of the enemy moving against them. And they don't just want to be defensive of their position, but they plan to take the fight to the enemy!"

"Do you think that they would go after innocent people to complete their goals?"

"Nothing or no one would be a problem for them, according to Leroy. If innocent people had to die for their case of justice, then they could live with that. People had grown soft after the 1960s Civil Rights Movement, giving in to all the demands of those black politicians and do-gooders just trying to make a name for themselves with the press. If God had wanted the races to be mixed, He would have made Adam white and Eve black, but according to the Bible, that didn't happen. Eve was formed from one of Adam's ribs, so she had to be the same race as he was. And then there were the Arabs and the Jews fighting all the time, and two World Wars fought because Hitler wanted to get rid of the Jews, homosexuals, and Gypsies. If everyone would just stick with their own race, everything would have been fine. That's the kind of things that Leroy believes."

"I'm not doubting you, Ruby, but how does Leroy justify being involved with Native Americans mixing with Caucasians? The red man and the white man—sounds like it would go against their basic beliefs of mixing the races and cultures together," Butch said.

"When he comes up against something like that, he just says it's OK to have an exception if it helps maintain the natural order of things. They don't always make sense, but they have this real hatred for the U.S. Government and any police department that doesn't see things their way. The Choctaw County government works with them, or at least that's what Leroy says."

"Here's what we're going to do, Ruby. We are going to see if Charlotte Phillips of The Jasmine Inn can put you and the kids up for a while until we can work some of these technical things out."

"I don't have any money for a fancy motel or anything like that. Leroy only gives me enough money for groceries and medicine, so I never have money for anything else."

"We'll figure out how to pay for your stay later, but I want you to pack a small suitcase for you and the kids, come with us now back to The Jasmine Inn, and we'll do the rest. We know someone who will pay for your stay at the bed and breakfast inn, so all you need to do is check in with the kids." Ruby reluctantly agreed to come with them, and within twenty minutes they were trampling back through the woods to Butch's pickup truck to take Ruby to the B&B. Butch and Claire agreed to meet the school bus and gather her three children for her and drop them off at The Jasmine Inn. Claire called ahead and spoke to Charlotte.

"Charlotte, we're going to need a little favor from you. We think we may have found a crack in the armor of that invisible cult that's operating in Choctaw County. We have convinced the wife of one of the members of the organization to leave her husband and go into hiding for a few days while we organize a raid on their camp. She has three small children, and they will all need a place to sleep and food to eat. I cannot promise you how soon we can get you reimbursed from the state of Alabama or the federal government for your trouble, but we will make sure you are finally whole once this thing is settled. Do you have room for them, and can you afford to let them stay with you for a week or so until we can get this cult dismantled?"

"Do you think that these are the same people who had my Charles murdered?"

"We do, but we're going to need a little time to prove it. If you'd rather us try to work out something else, we will. For reasons I can't elaborate on right now, we don't know who in the county government that we can trust. The sheriff, Judge Doran, and the coroner are all subjects of interest, but that's all we know at this point. The sheriff's office is paying for our stay, but if we ask him to shelter Ruby Smithson and her three kids, and assuming he is involved in the cover-up going on in Choctaw County, they will be at risk. It's totally your decision. You could be put in danger if Ruby's husband figures out what's going on and tried to come after them. You should know that up front." Without hesitation, Charlotte spoke firmly.

"You bring them over here whenever you need to do so. I'll take care of them for as long as we need to until you get this cult thing figured out. As far as being afraid of Leroy Smithson and his cultists, I have a nice Mossberg 590 Shockwave pump action 12-gauge shotgun that Charles had before he was murdered. He taught me how to use it, and I can take out six bad guys without reloading it. It won't be the first time I've defended myself from people trying to cause me harm." Claire was surprised that Charlotte even knew what a 12-guage shotgun was capable of, much less the knowledge of which one she had and how many rounds it would hold. Claire was impressed and chuckled a little to herself.

"We have Ruby in the pickup right now, and we intend to intercept the kids when they get off the school bus this afternoon. Leroy works out at the mill, so he normally gets off around 3:30 PM or 4:00 PM, and we have been told that he usually stops by the tavern for a beer or two before he heads home. That should give us enough time to corral the kids, get them safely to you and The Jasmine Inn, reunited them with their mother, and confront Leroy while there's no one else around to get hurt. At least, that's our goal. If Leroy puts up a fuss, both Butch and I are armed as well, and we are pretty good shots!"

"Can you do that legally?"

"Our boss back in Ashburn is good friends with the governor, and we are going to ask him to see if the Alabama Attorney General will issue us temporary authority to act on the behalf of his office as special agents. It's a win-win for everyone involved. Butch called him just a few minutes ago and we should know soon if we are legitimate or rouge. Either way, we're going to try to interrupt this cult stuff going on in Choctaw County."

"You bring all the Smithson family over here, and I promise you that I will take care of them. Don't worry about the cost of housing and feeding them, because I have a little reserve money left from the insurance settlement when Charles died. I can't think of a better way to invest it than to bring an end to that terrible invisible cult operating at will in Choctaw County!"

"Ruby is being very brave to step out and do the right thing, and we don't want anything but good to come out of this for her." Claire said that so Ruby would be reassured that she could trust Butch and her as they went after her self-righteous husband.

"I'll be ready for them when you get here," Charlotte said, and the line went dead.

"Is that the lady who owns The Jasmine Inn?" Ruby asked. "That's mighty nice of her taking care of us that way, especially since I think the cult had something to do with her husband's death."

"Don't mention anything to her about her husband or anything else to do with the cult, unless she asks you something specific. She's a very kind and nice lady, and she will help you and the kids get through this mess."

"What about school for the kids? Should I keep them out until this is settled?"

"Since this is Friday, and I think Monday is a national holiday, which will give us three full days to bring this investigation to a head, and we think things should be back to normal by then. However, don't send the kids back to school until we tell you that it's safe," Butch said.

"OK. I'll do as you say. I'm just afraid when Leroy finds out that I'm gone and that I've taken the kids, there'll be no going back."

"Let us worry about that, Ruby. We just want you and your kids safe while all of this is going down."

"If you can get rid of that judge, he's the worst of the lot!"

"Are you talking about Judge Louis Doran? What makes you say that?"

"Because before every mission that Leroy went on, he got a personal call from the judge with instructions as to what was expected of him. Leroy has a bad temper, and he doesn't attend church on Sundays, but deep down inside I believe that he is a good man. He never beat me or the kids until he got involved with that cult and Judge Doran. Then something just snapped, and he became a different man overnight."

"We will work things out and try to get your old Leroy back to you as before. We can't promise you anything, because he has made claims that the cult will fight to the death, like the Ruby Ridge cult in Texas a few years ago, but we will try to take him alive."

"I still love the man I married, but that's not Leroy right now. The kids and I are afraid of him, and we go to bed wondering if we will still be alive when the morning comes. People shouldn't have to live that way, especially little kids."

"We just need to get you and your children to a safe place until we can work through all of this," Butch said. They were pulling up into the circular driveway that was one of the features of the old Victorian house. Ruby's eyes were as big as saucers as she took in all the gingerbread woodwork that was prevalent on the front porch and around all of the windows in the bed and breakfast inn.

"This place is beautiful," Ruby said. "It's like something out of a magazine. Is the owner going to let me and my kids stay here until everything blows over?" she asked.

"Yep," Claire said. "Now let me and Butch help you with your bags and the stuff you brought for your kids." Charlotte was standing on the front porch in a sign of welcome to her new guest, and she showed Ruby to a room on the second floor of the old mansion.

"Charlotte, you have probably figured out by now that Claire and I don't use one of the bedrooms that the Choctaw County sheriff's office is paying for," Butch said. He blushed a little, but Charlotte didn't seem to notice or care, and Butch continued with what he was going to say. "Why don't you let the kids or Ruby use our unused room. That way, the county will be paying for some of your expenses without them even knowing. Keep your ledger of expenses as if Ruby wasn't using our extra room, and we will see that you eventually get reimbursed for all your expenses when this is settled."

"That's nice of you, Butch. I can do that. As far as you and Claire using only one bedroom, that's none of my business. You're both adults of a consenting age, and I try not to get into other people's business, unless it's something like this with Ruby and her kids. There are six bedrooms in this house, not counting the owner's suite, and I can put the kids in a bedroom upstairs next to their mother. She may be able to corral them into not destroying my antiques if she's near them!" Charlotte smiled and Butch gave her a thumbs-up signal. Butch and Claire said their goodbyes to Ruby, promised to fetch her kids to the B&B after the bus took them to their normal drop off point near their cabin in the woods, and they slipped out of The Jasmine Inn. They had other fish to fry before picking up the kids.

Chapter 13

Taking a Chance

"Butch, how well do you think Sam Hannity knows Sheriff Conrad Phillips?" Claire asked.

"I don't know. Why do you ask," Butch answered with a question on his face.

"Well, if someone had accused you of something as bad as being a party to such criminal activity as extortion, theft, and murder, even knowing you for only a couple of years, I wouldn't believe a word of it. If Sam has known Sheriff Phillips for many years, maybe he can give us some insight as to what is going on in Choctaw County."

"And you think he will be totally openminded in his opinion?"

"I don't know, Butch. But if the sheriff is a good guy, he can help us take down this cult."

"True, but if he's part of it, he can wreck our entire plan and take us down with its failure to find and destroy such a bad operation. It's a touchy question, don't you think?"

"How well do you trust our mayor?"

"Claire, I've only known the mayor about the same amount of time as you. What do you think of our mayor?" Claire wasn't ready for Butch to turn the tables on her, so she was startled that she had to answer the same question she had posed to Butch.

"As far as I have knowledge, Sam Hannity is a good guy. He seems to be honest, loyal, and legitimate, but so do most of the crooks out there ripping off the general public," Claire said.

"In other words, you have no idea if he's clean or dirty?"

"Exactly. If I were to guess, which is a bad habit to have in our business, I would say he's clean. I doubt he's ever taken a pencil box from a fellow grade-schooler."

"That's an unusual comparison," Claire said.

"Well, I guess it's confession time," Butch laughed. "My father broke me from being a thief the only way one can do that. When I was a kid in the first grade, we were poor and didn't have money for things that weren't necessary. The building where I was assigned was one big room, with a cloak room for coats, goulashes, and raincoats. One day when I was hanging up my coat, I saw the neatest pencil box sticking out of the pocket of another coat. It wasn't fancy by today's standards, but it was something that I had envied of other students, but my folks refused to buy one for me. Without thinking about possible consequences, I put the pencil box in my own coat, took my seat in the classroom, and acted like nothing had happened. When I got home, I was playing with it when my mother asked me about it. I lied to her and said it somehow got into my coat by mistake. She didn't make a big fuss about it, so I thought that I had gotten away with the theft. When my father arrived home from work, my mother must have told him about our conversation, and he confronted me about it. I loved my mother, but I feared my father for good reason. After the truth came out, he whipped me with his leather belt, made me go to the teacher the next day and apologize to the student I stole from, and to the whole class for being a thief. Even for a six-year-old, it was a very embarrassing and humiliating experience. Other than inadvertently taking pens and pencils from work, I have never stolen anything knowingly since that time."

"I'm sure that there's a reason for you confiding such an embarrassing experience to me, but somehow I may have missed it," Claire said.

"A thief is a thief; a liar is a liar; and the age of the person committing the crime is incidental to the act itself. If Sam is a liar or thief, we wouldn't know that easily, especially if he had been doing it since he was a young boy. Conversely, if he had parents like mine, and he learned right from wrong at a young age, then he'd probably follow those instincts the rest of his life. That's what I'm betting on. I think we can trust Sam. The real question is whether or not he can trust his friend the sheriff."

"I'll let you call Sam. Maybe you guys will be more honest with each other if a woman is not involved," Claire said. Butch gave her one of his knowing looks—knowing that she was passing the buck once more! He dialed the number and waited for it to be answered.

"Ashburn City Hall," the voice said. "How may I help you?"

"This is Chief Butch Todd, is the mayor available?"

"Sure, Butch. Let me locate him." It took a few minutes to get connected with Sam Hannity, but he eventually picked up the receiver and addressed Butch by name.

"Butch? How are you and your Chief of Detectives doing out there in Choctaw County?"

"Well, Mayor, that's one reason we are calling you." There was silence on the phone for a minute for the mayor to get his bearings, and then he asked the obvious question.

"You're where the action is, Butch. How can I be helpful to you and Claire? Have you helped the sheriff figure out what's going on over there? I would have figured that you two would be on your way to Gulf Shores by now."

"We have a rather sensitive question to ask you, Mayor. Please don't take offense, but we need to know what you think about Sheriff Conrad Phillips' character. Do you think money or influence would be attractive enough to allow him to turn his head and ignore illegal activity happening in his county?"

"I'm at a loss at your question, Butch. What makes you ask such a question about the sheriff?" Butch could tell that he had hit a nerve with Mayor Hannity.

"We're not accusing him or anyone else in Choctaw County of anything at the present time, but there appears to be a major conspiracy taking place over here, and both Claire and I are of the opinion that what is happening would be hard to perpetuated itself without some inside government help and support. The circuit judge, coroner, and possibly other paid official government employees may be involved. At first, we discounted the possibility of Sheriff Phillips being involved, but there are rumors that indicate the opposite. We want to give him the benefit of the doubt, and we could really use his help to bring this cult to justice, but if he's involved with the bad players, it could be disastrous to us, and some other people involved in exposing the cult members. That's why it is so important to know for sure if your friend is on the good side of this situation, but we can't ask him and count on his answer to be truthful. Anyway, he'd probably be pissed if he thought we even suspected him of being dirty. There are some people who have died already mysteriously, and we don't want to add to that total."

"It looks like I sent you to into the briar patch, doesn't it? I'm sorry if that is the case. What can I do on my end to help?"

"Do you have a good relationship with Sheriff Phillips?"

"I think so, but who really knows people these days? Do you want me to confront him?"

"Yes, but let's figure out how to do it so we won't be too exposed."

"How has he treated you and Claire?"

"We couldn't ask for much more cooperation, but we haven't made much use of his voluntary help since we were told he might be in on the conspiracy. He could be of immense help, assuming we knew we could trust him fully."

"Give me an hour to contact and speak to the sheriff, and then call me back in precisely one hour." Butch looked at his watch and saw that it was 2:00 PM, and he agreed. They would be picking up the Smithson kids at 3:30 PM, so they needed to get this settled as soon as possible. If the sheriff were clean, he could help them hide Ruby and her kids more effectively.

"I will call you at 3:00 PM. We must intercept and pick up three little kids from their bus stop without their father getting wind of it. They are usually getting off the bus around 3:30 PM, so we will be running close on time." Butch was trying to encourage the mayor to make sure he was not late getting back to them.

"I'll call you sooner, if possible, and let you know what I find out." The mayor hung up, and Butch told Claire what he had said. They had about an hour and a half to kill, so they decided to go to Lulu's Diner and see if she had any new gossip for them. As they pulled up in front of Lulu's, she came out of the diner and got into Butch' truck.

"Will you please drive around back?" Butch and Claire looked at her in disbelief. She had never been this forward or friendly. They wondered what had changed to make Lulu change her approach to them so different. Butch did as she asked, and he pulled into a narrow alley which ran along the back of the storefronts on Main Street.

"What's going on, Lulu?" Claire asked.

"Leroy Smithson was in the restaurant looking for his wife earlier today. He came in with three or four other men from the mill, so I didn't think anything about it at first. He's never been very friendly, doesn't bring his family to town at all, and rarely steps into my restaurant. However, today when I was pouring them all coffee, he asked me if I had seen his wife, Ruby. When I told him I hadn't seen her for months, he looked troubled and mean. They had their coffee, ate a quick lunch, and all left together. I didn't get the impression that Leroy was going back to work at the mill today. Just a hunch, but I know these people well and I got the impression he was going to go looking for his wife."

"Did he or any of this thug friends ask about us?" Claire asked.

"No, and that surprised me a little bit. He knows that you and Butch are the only new people in town, and he's probably heard all the rumors about you being here to investigate the cult activity in the county. It's one of the most popular rumors in Butler currently."

"We are going to tell you something in confidence, Ruby, but you must promise not to share what we tell you with *anyone* in town. Will you promise us that?" Butch asked.

"Sure, Butch. What is it?"

"We have hidden Ruby from Leroy, and we intend grab the kids when they get off the school bus at 3:30 PM, and we will reunite Ruby with her kids at that time. We're afraid that if Ruby and the kids are underfoot when the pressure is put on Leroy to surrender or go to jail, he may react and start shooting. We don't want any other innocents to be harmed while this cult thing is cleared up."

"That's probably a good idea. What can I do to help?"

"Do you have a cell phone?"

"Doesn't everyone have one today?" she laughed. Claire gave her a business card and asked her to text or call her if she saw Leroy back in town before 3:30 PM.

"If he's in town, he can't impede us from snatching his kids."

"Great idea. Anything else I can do?" Butch hesitated, but then he asked her about Sheriff Phillips.

"Lulu, how well do you know Sheriff Conrad Phillips?"

"Pretty good, I guess. Why?"

"Claire and I believe that some prominent government people are mixed up in this invisible cult thing operating in the county. If you think about it, how could they get away with everything that has happened unless people in power are looking the other way? You probably know that Charles Phillips' death was questionable, and that the coroner didn't allow an autopsy following his mysterious death."

"I had heard something about that, but I didn't think any more about it."

"Not only that, but Judge Louis Doran has been suspected to have been giving light sentences to some of the members of the cult when they get caught committing some heinous crimes. We've also been told that the judge runs the show between the cult and what they do as a group. It would not surprise me if he were not a member of the cult himself," Butch said.

"Wow, that's a lot to think about. How are you going to get to the bottom of things if everyone at the top is controlling what happens?"

"That's why we're asking about the sheriff. Our boss back in Ashburn has known Sheriff Phillips for many years and he doesn't think that Phillips is dirty. What is your opinion?"

"I too have known Sheriff Phillips for many years. I have voted for him each time he has run for Choctaw County Sheriff for one basic reason."

"And what might that reason be, Lulu?"

"The very first time Conrad Phillips ran for office as the sheriff, he said that he would not hire his friends and family just because he had the power to do so, but rather that he would hire the most qualified person for each position which came open in his office. His first hire was a new secretary, because the one who had been working for the previous sheriff was his daughter, and Conrad knew that having an old adversary working within a few feet of you all day probably wouldn't be a wise move. So, he advertised for the opening, interviewed a bunch of men and women for the job, and wound-up hiring Mattlyn Stone, a young woman who had previously been a schoolteacher for the sixth grade. She was going to take a leave of absence from teaching for a while, and she promised Conrad that she would work a minimum of four years if he hired her. Since his term was only for four years, she took the job. She wasn't related to him, she wasn't a best friend of the family, and he really had never met her before he interviewed her, but she was an excellent typist, could file well, and minded her business. She was paid to do a job, and she did that job without meddling in the sheriff's business affairs. When he ran for reelection and won again, he asked her to stay on and she agreed. That was sixteen years ago. That story may sound simple to you, but he's been consistent his entire career, as far as I can see."

"You've never heard that he was complicit in that invisible cult operating in the shadows of Choctaw County?"

"The sheriff drives a ten-year-old pickup truck, wears off-the-rack suits from Sears or J.C. Penny's, and probably has never owned a fancy pair of shoes. He thinks that a 'black tie' event is simply wearing a black tie with a suit. I'm not saying that he's perfect, but I cannot imagine him abandoning his oath of office for any amount of money in the form of a bribe or special favors directed toward him."

"What do you think about Judge Louis Doran? Do you think that he has the same type of integrity as your sheriff?" Claire asked. Lulu shook her head and made a surprising comment.

"I wouldn't trust that judge as far as I could throw him with one arm, and as fat as he is, that wouldn't be too far," Lulu laughed. "There may be some honest people in our local government offices, but I doubt Judge Doran is one of them. I've overheard several of my diners saying that the judge has a lot of influence on those people in the cult, and he keeps things over them to keep them in line. I don't know if it's true, and I don't know what it means, but it doesn't sound good to me." Butch and Claire thanked Lulu for her input, and they drove her back around the front of Lulu's Diner and let her out of their truck.

"Lulu, thank you for your help in all of this craziness," Claire said, and she patted her on her hand as she exited the truck.

"I'll let you know of I see Leroy Smithson. I'm telling you that he is a bad seed!" Lulu said as she walked away and back into her restaurant. They thanked her again, and they drove off toward the western side of town to try and get to the bus before Leroy figured everything out. They parked off the side of the road that led to the Smithson's house and where Ruby said that the bus driver let the kids off each day for their walk into the woods and their cabin. They saw the big yellow bus heading their way when Claire's cell phone rang. She recognized the number from Lulu's Diner. Claire picked up and confirmed her best guess.

"I just wanted you to know that I saw Leroy going into the hardware store a few minutes ago. I imagine he will be headed home soon, so you had better get whatever business you intend to do done out towards his house and move on. If he spots you two lurking around his cabin, he will add things up and think you might be one of the reasons he can't find his wife."

"Great idea, Lulu," Claire said, and they saw the three kids get off the bus and head in their direction. Ruby had written a note for Claire and Butch to show to the kids, and shared a secret safety password, so they would know to trust Butch and Claire. Butch showed them his detective shield, the letter from their mother, and said "peanut butter" to them. They all got into the backseat of Butch's pickup truck, and they all rode off toward The Jasmine House B&B.

Chapter 14

Some Friendly Assistance

After reuniting the kids with Ruby, Claire and Butch decided that they had to push their investigation forward as quickly as possible. Beside knowing that Leroy Smithson was known for being a hothead and totally unpredictable, he also had some violent history with his wife and children, according to Ruby. They had not heard back from Mayor Hannity, and his opinion was a key element going forward in their investigation. He was going to speak directly with his old friend, Sheriff Conrad Phillips, and then he was going to call Butch and Claire back and give them advice about how to move forward. It was now after 4:00 PM and Butch and Claire expected Leroy was getting riled up about his wife and kids not being at home where he normally expected them at this time in the afternoon. Butch and Claire had just gotten the children settled into The Jasmine House and Charlotte had promised the kids fried chicken and mashed potatoes for dinner, so she was busy preparing the evening meal. While Charlotte had a few rooms vacant in The Jasmine House, she didn't want to expose anyone else to any possible dangers from Leroy Smithson and his invisible cult members, so she would simply tell anyone interested in renting a room that she had no availability at the present time. Although this might cost her some needed revenue, she trusted that Butch and Claire would get her some financial relief once everything was settled with their investigation. They had told her as much. Butch had asked Ruby to meet with Charlotte, Claire, and him on the wraparound front porch before dinnertime so they could discuss what might happen next with the investigation. She agreed, and the four of them were sitting in rocking chairs, sipping on sweet tea, and discussing all the possible outcomes of Butch's and Claire's daring decision to separate Ruby and her children from Leroy Smithson. His reputation for violence had everyone concerned for Ruby and the kids' health, but things were coming to a head and Butch didn't think it would be wise to leave four innocent people in the middle of what might turn out to be a firefight. Leroy had pretty much already said that he would not be taken alive if the authorities came on his property to arrest him, and no one knew what he might do to his children if things came to a head. No one knew exactly how many members of the invisible cult were, and Butch and Claire didn't want to chance Leroy's family getting injured or killed because he decided that he wanted to go out in a blaze of glory.

"Ruby, I think we need to discuss what happens next in our pursuit of shutting down the invisible cult in which your husband is a member. Our first responsibility is to keep you and your children safe from all possible harm which could come to you if you are caught in a crossfire between your husband and the police. Once that matter is settled, there's the possibility of talking Leroy into surrendering to the authorities, giving up his fellow co-conspirators, and having this matter solved peacefully. Those are our goals. We believe we have been successful in isolating you and your children from the worst of what may come, but the other things fall squarely on Leroy's shoulders. Do you think he will listen to reason, or do you think he will react like he's done before and attacked the messenger?" Butch asked. Ruby sat quietly contemplating Butch's question before she answered.

"I don't know my husband anymore. When we first married, he was a little gruff and rough around the edges, but he was kind and generous to me and the kids as they came along. However, a few years ago he was invited to a secret meeting of this club which meets in the forest not too far from our cabin, and he joined up with a ragtag bunch of folks who were angry with the government for taking the Native Americans' land, letting carpetbaggers destroy all the good things that existed prior to the South losing the Civil War, and any other person with a personal grudge against the United States Government. From what little he has shared with me, there aren't that many of them in the group, but they are all devoted to their cause. I doubt any of them will surrender peacefully."

"Did Leroy tell you how many members of his cult were active and ready to fight the government?" Claire asked.

"He only said that they had mortars and rockets, bombs and explosives, and that if the government came for any of them, the others would attack the Choctaw County Courthouse and kill everyone inside as punishment for what had been done to all of them over the years."

"Did he say whether or not they had automatic weapons?" Butch asked.

"Yeah, he would often brag that they had an arsenal which would let them hold off a small army for days or weeks, and that they would kill ten people to one of their own murdered by the government."

"Do you have any idea of where their safehouse may be?" Claire asked. Ruby put her head into her hands and began to weep. It took a few minutes to calm her back down, but Claire eventually managed to get Ruby to stop crying long enough to tell her an important fact about the cult.

"That's why I was willing to leave my home and take my kids away from all of that violence. Leroy has never admitted it, but I think he has built a fortress underground in our backyard, and he often had members of his cult over and they disappeared for hours into the woods behind our house. I watched them a couple of times, but they just seemed to disappear when they were fifty to sixty feet from our back door. I can only assume that he dug a cellar or underground bunker, but I've never tried looking for it. Leroy told me and the kids to never go into the woods behind the house because it was very dangerous, and we might get killed. That's all he said, but I knew something bad was going on there. I just never had the courage to leave him or the house until you two came along." Ruby started crying again.

"Ruby, you are safe with us, and Charlotte will protect you here as long as you need to stay," Claire reassured her as Ruby continued to weep quietly. Butch's phone rang and he could see that the call was from Mayor Sam Hannity. He excused himself from the three women, walked down the steps to the sidewalk, and put himself outside of hearing range of the front porch. Once he answered the phone, he was relieved.

"Butch, this is Sam Hannity. I spoke with Sheriff Phillips, and he is as solid as I've ever known him to be. He told me that a man named Leroy Smithson approached him and told the sheriff that the county circuit judge and some other elected officials were on board with eliminating the unsavory people in Choctaw County, and they wanted to know which side the sheriff was going to take. Without details of any illegal activity, Sheriff Phillips could only take a positive stance against vigilante justice, and he told Leroy that he could not be a part of anything illegal or harmful to those people who had elected him to his office. Leroy laughed at him, made a veiled threat, and that's the last thing he's heard from anyone in the cult personally. However, he thought that the death of Charles Phillips, no relationship to the sheriff, was suspicious, and he requested that the local coroner perform an autopsy on his body. However, legally the coroner has the authority to permit or refuse such a request, and he refused it. He declared that Charles Phillips had died of natural causes, even though he was less than 50 years old and had passed a physical with no serious diagnosis for diseases just a few months before his death. The sheriff went to Judge Louis Doran demanding that the body be exhumed and autopsied, but the judge sided with the coroner and warned Sheriff Phillips to mind his own business if he wanted to get reelected to his position as sheriff. With no one to help his case, Conrad made notes of his conversations with the judge and the coroner, as well as a couple of secret voice tapes with his cell phone and was waiting for an opportunity to reopen the case. He had spoken to Charlotte Phillips, Charles' wife and the innkeeper of The Jasmine House, on numerous occasions, but they simply had no evidence of wrongdoing by the judge, the coroner, or anyone else in Butler. Therefore, the investigation became a cold case, and that's where it stands today." Butch thanked Sam for his input, hung up his phone, and walked back to the front porch of The Jasmine House.

"Ruby and Charlotte, will you please excuse me and Claire for a few moments? We will join you in the house for dinner when it's ready, but we need to talk about a few things before that happens." They agreed, left the front porch to the two detectives, and Butch repeated what Sam had just told him about the sheriff.

"It sounds like we may have interpreted the facts incorrectly thinking that Sheriff Phillips may have been on the other side of this nefarious situation," Claire said. "What do you think we should do now?"

"You and I need to pay an unofficial visit to Sheriff Conrad Phillips at his home or some other less public place than the Choctaw County Courthouse. I'll call him and set it up." Butch dialed the sheriff's private phone number, reached him at home, and explained that he and Claire needed to sit down with the sheriff and clear the air. Butch asked the sheriff if he had an out-of-the-way place in mind for such a meeting, and the sheriff gave them directions to his fishing pier on Mosley Lake, just off Highway 25. Conrad gave them specific directions of where to park and how to get to his dock on foot. It was 4:30 PM and they only had an hour or two before dark, Butch told Charlotte that he and Claire would have her warm them up a plate of food when they had returned from an emergency meeting. They didn't give her any details, and she didn't ask. In less than ten minutes, they were headed for Mosley Lake, just a few miles south of Butler.

The trip to Mosley Lake took only ten minutes, but finding the remote cabin took another twenty. They spotted a small cabin, a four-wheeler, and a dock with a man resembling Sheriff Phillips casting a line and attempting to catch his dinner. When he saw them, he reeled in his bait, waved his visitors towards his pier, and welcomed them with a handshake.

"I was wondering how your investigation was going the past few days, but I didn't want to intrude. Sam told me that both of you were crackerjack detectives, so I didn't want to get in your way," Conrad said.

"I think we need to do some explaining to you, Sheriff," Butch said. Sheriff Phillips looked skeptical and was quiet a moment before answering.

"I'm not sure I'm following you, Butch. What are you not telling me?"

"Did you get to speak to our boss, Mayor Hannity, a little while ago?"

"I did, and to be honest, I'm not sure why he was calling me. He said something to me about the invisible cult that we're all looking for. While he was curious about a few things, he never really asked me anything about my personal knowledge about where they might be hiding."

"We were told that you might be involved with Judge Doran and the coroner in covering up some of the irregularities in the deaths and reporting of them officially. What we heard was obviously bad information, but we had to be sure whose side you were on before we brought you into our investigation. I hope you can understand our initial reluctance to include you," Butch said, hoping that the sheriff would take the slight without getting angry. Conrad began to laugh, and now Butch and Claire were the ones confused.

"We were afraid you would be upset with us, and we're glad to see that you see humor in everything," Claire said. Conrad sighed as if a large load was lifted off his shoulders before he answered.

"It isn't so much that I think there is humor in what these conspirators are doing in my county, but the irony is that they are the ones who are destroying the very freedoms which they think that they are protecting by attacking the government. A few of the things that they are upset about are reasonable, but unfortunately when you live in a society where everyone must get along, everyone must make a few adjustments and compromises so we can all live together in peace. Most of those hiding in the woods and participating in the actions of their invisible cult have no idea what they're fighting for now. There were those Native Americans who were treated poorly by the unscrupulous

Northern carpetbaggers, politicians who used their position with the government to seize private property and old plantations for their own profit, cutting the heirs of the land out of any right of possession of their property, and wealthy merchants who bought up property and houses for ten cents on the dollar. Many people believe that Abraham Lincoln was assassinated not because of the slavery issue, but by his own political allies who found out that he planned to be generous and forgiving to the conquered South. Political historians tell us that there's no way he would have allowed the kinds of things that went on during the reconstruction of the Southern states from 1865 until 1877. The lack of leadership from the White House and the federal government was one reason the racial split in the country was so dramatic, and why the so-called White Supremacists and the KKK even had a chance of getting rooted in the South. Following those issues, forced integration in the 1960s was looked at as just another government takeover of state's rights. How the Choctaw Indians and the KKK were able to forge a cooperative agreement is beyond me."

"It sounds like you've given a lot of thought to these issues," Claire said. She was impressed that Conrad was a deep thinker, and not just a good old boy who was elected because he was popular and a white man.

"How can I help you two get this mess cleaned up once and for all?" Conrad asked. Butch told the sheriff about snatching up Ruby Smithson and her three children and stashing them at The Jasmine Inn. He also asked the sheriff if he could help Charlotte cover her expenses since she was acting in a protective manner for the benefit of citizens of Choctaw County.

"You can reassure her that we will make her whole financially for assisting us in protecting the Smithson family. I will also write her a thank you note when this is all over."

"Charlotte just wants the truth to come out about Charles and the true cause of his death. She is convinced that he was murdered by someone in the cult because of what happened to their convicted cult member and how he died in prison. She is sure it was a revenge murder."

"She is probably more correct than she knows," Conrad said.

"How do you plan to get this eventually cleaned up, and how can my office help you?"

"How well do you know your staff, Sheriff?" Claire asked.

"I'm not sure what you're asking, Claire."

"Do you think you may have some officers who are sympathetic to the cult members?"

"It's possible, but I doubt it. Half of my staff is either Native American or African American, and they don't tolerate any discrimination in the ranks. I have a captain who is black, a lieutenant who is a Choctaw Indian, and three Hispanic patrol officers. We only have ten peace officers, other than me, so that's half of the force who are minorities. I imagine they would know if someone in their ranks is a racist. Maybe I'm just too trusting," he said and chuckled.

"I doubt that, Sheriff. It sounds like you know exactly what is going on in your office," Butch said.

"Why is that important?" Conrad asked.

"We need to have a well-trained armed force to smoke out these cultists when we decide to make our move.

We can ask the governor's office and the Alabama Attorney General to get involved if you think it's necessary. It's your police precinct, therefore, your call," Butch said. Conrad thought for a minute and then suggested that it would be nice to have the Alabama Highway Patrol as backups, assuming they need them, but that he really preferred to keep the federal government out of their county business.

"That works for us," Claire said. "Now let's make some plans to wipe this cult out as soon as possible." Everyone agreed.

Chapter 15

Unwitting Helper

The very last thing Leroy Smithson ever thought he would do is become a traitor to his own cause, but survival always comes before idealism. Leroy had been stopped by one of the local police officers and was requested to join him in his cruiser. While it was a bit unusual, it wasn't a stretch to think that the local constabulary might want the input of local citizens from time to time. Leroy didn't hesitate to join the officer, but then noticed Sheriff Conrad Phillips sitting in the backseat behind him. Leroy's danger signals began to blare in his ears.

"What's this all about?" he asked the police officer, ignoring the sheriff as if he weren't sitting there. Sheriff Phillips had not uttered a word.

"Leroy, I think the sheriff may want to have a word with you," and he waited for Phillips to speak from the backseat.

"Leroy, you and I need to have an honest conversation that may not please you," he said. "We know you are involved with the invisible cult that operates in Choctaw County, and it's time we came to an understanding."

"I'm not sure what you're talking about, Sheriff," Leroy mumbled. "I was just minding my business when your officer picked me up." Then his comment went very wrong. "You know, it's not illegal to be a white man in Choctaw County going about one's personal business." The sheriff waited for that comment to settle before he confronted Leroy with some very serious facts.

"I'm going to tell you some things, and I'm only going to tell you once, so you'd better listen up. Your wife and kids are being held in protective custody, and most likely be relocated to another area by the U.S. Marshal Service. If you don't cooperate with us, you not only will be prosecuted to the full extent of the law, but you may never see your family again. Are you listening?" He paused to guarantee that he had Leroy's attention.

"You can't kidnap my family and use them against me!" he protested. The sheriff chuckled before he spoke again.

"Leroy, Ruby asked us for protection, and included the kids in her request. She hoped you would join her in the WITSEC program so you can live a normal life once more. She is terrified of the invisible cult and what it might do to her and the kids." Leroy thought for a minute before he spoke.

"I'm not under arrest? I can get out of this car and just walk away?"

"Yes, you can make that decision, Leroy," the sheriff said. "However, your arsenal in the woods in no longer available to you. It's been seized by the ATF as a potential crime scene. It appears that many unauthorized firearms, ammunition, and other contraband was found buried on your property. The land is subject forfeiture due to the seriousness of the criminal activity discovered there, so you will need to go somewhere else." There was another period of silence from Leroy. He wasn't the brightest bulb in the box, but he was no dummy either.

"What would I have to do to surrender to you? What would you want from me?"

"Here's what we have to offer you, assuming you are fully cooperative and honest with us," the sheriff said. "We will instruct the U.S. Marshal Service to put you and your entire family into witness protection, given new identities, relocated to another area of the country, given jobs, and other assistance."

"What do I have to do to get that kind of a deal?"

"We need to know all the names of the members of your secret cult, their plans, and where they keep their weapons and ammunition. You will eventually need to return to Butler to testify against them in a court of law." This time Leroy was the once chuckling. "Do you find that humorous, Leroy?"

"Judge Doran is a guilty as the rest of us. You'll never get a conviction of the cult members while Judge Doran is a sitting judge in this county."

"We know, Leroy. There are things going on behind the scenes at high government levels which will correct that situation, but you don't have to worry about those details. The trial which will take place will be held in federal court, not a state or county court. The crimes that will be prosecuted carry long federal prison sentences, and some possibly the death penalty. You will be escorted into and out of court from your hidden location by federal marshals, so there will be little danger to you or your family. Your alternative is the loss of your family forever, a possible long sentence in a federal correctional facility, and who knows what the cult will do to you when we put it out on the street that you have cooperated, whether you cooperate or not." Leroy had lost his smirk and sarcasm and was looking like a lost ball in high weeds.

"You can't do that! You can't lie."

"Why not," the sheriff laughed. "We can do all kinds of things to get to the truth, so you should play ball with us. Otherwise, you're going to become some big guy's girlfriend when you go to prison."

"How long can I think about it?" Sheriff Phillips looked at his watch.

"I'll give you two minutes. Otherwise, we are going to let you out of this car, and then we'll immediately put the word out on the street that you have become an informer for the police department." Phillips looked again at this watch, and then said, "time's up. What's you decision?"

"I guess I don't have much of a choice, do I?"

"Not the way I see it. Now, let's go back to the station and start from the beginning."

"If the other members of our group see me with you, they will think I've turned on them. My life won't be worth a plugged nickel."

"If you tell us what we need to know, every detail that you can remember, we will reunite you with Ruby, Terrence, Karen, and Joey by nightfall. Otherwise, things are going to get bad for you, Leroy," the sheriff said.

"I'll tell you everything. Can I at least go back and get my personal stuff from the house when we're done here?"

"That's not a good idea, Leroy. I'll have an officer bring you some clothes, toothbrush, razor, and things like that from your house. Otherwise, we will replace what you leave behind. You will have a new identity, new wardrobe, and new friends. However, there is one caveat to our offer," he said. Conrad got right up into the personal space of Leroy's face before he spoke. "If I ever hear again about you slapping your wife and kids around, I'll come looking for you, and I will find you. Do you understand me?" Leroy answered in a small voice.

"Yes, sir. I understand, and it will not happen again."

"It better not happen again, or I'm going to put this size eleven boot up your ass. Got it?" the sheriff was breathing down Leroy's collar.

"I've got it." Conrad let go of Leroy's shirt, and he sank back down into the seat like a wounded animal. "I just want another chance to start over with my family." They arrived back at the sheriff's office and Leroy walked inside without being handcuffed. Conrad put Leroy in a soundproof interviewing room, gave him a bottle of water, and locked the door behind him. The room had a one-way mirror for observation purposes, and Leroy had attracted a crowd of onlookers hoping to see the sheriff take Leroy down a couple of notches. Leroy had been disrespectful of several of the deputies, and no one cared much for anyone associated with that secret cult that met out in the woods and did terrible things to people who they didn't like or respect.

"Okay, guys. Let's move along. There's nothing to see here," Conrad said to his deputies. All the sheriff's people respected him, and when he asked them to move along, they did. The sheriff took Mattlyn Stone, his personal secretary, into the interrogation room and had her write down everything that Leroy shared with them. After an hour, the sheriff gave Leroy a bathroom break, and he was escorted down the hall to a men's room. Mattlyn looked at the sheriff and just shook her head. The amount of information which Leroy was sharing was unimaginable.

He listed local businesses, many of his fellow workers at the mill, and of course Judge Doran as accomplices of threats to businesses, extortion, and some murders. Leroy explained that the Choctaw Indians associated with the cult were not really members, but they had felt abused by having their land seized by the government, and they helped hide weapons and ammunition for the cultists. Leroy told Conrad that when the white members of the invisible cult were arrested and put into jail, that he thought the Native Americans associating with the white men would simply disappear into the thick woods that surrounded Butler and Choctaw County. When the sheriff thought that he had extracted all the important information which Leroy could share about the invisible cult, he instructed one of his officers to deliver Leroy to The Jasmine House so he could be reunited with his wife and kids. He thought Leroy was going to cry. Before he left, the sheriff warned Leroy one more time about physically abusing his wife and kids.

"If you need to get anger management counseling, or any other psychological help to prevent you from harming your family, you just need to tell me. I can make that happen. But don't you *ever* strike any of them again!"

"I promise. I won't. I'm just glad that I can start again."

"You keep thinking that way, Leroy, and we'll all get along just fine." The last thing Sheriff Phillips saw was Leroy nodding his head vigorously that he had been cured of hurting those whom he loved. Only time would tell if he really was cured of his hateful ways, but he knew that he would be under a microscope for many days and weeks to come, so he had better get his act together.

* * *

The sheriff had gathered all his men together in the conference room, including Butch and Claire, and a dozen Alabama State Highway Patrolmen. Since it was evident that the county judge had controlled much of the illegal activities which had been going on for some time in Choctaw County, Sheriff had to petition the Alabama State AG to get involved in the takedown of Judge Doran, the local police chief of Butler, as well as the county coroner's office. All these men had been complicit in the extortion and blackmailing plots which had kept the local business owners quiet and in line with the judge's wishes.

"I'm glad to report to you all that we have two detectives with us who have the ear of the governor's office." By now all the local police personnel knew that Claire and Butch were the detectives Conrad were referring to, and the AHP were figuring it out as well. A loud sound of clapping hands greeted them, and they both appeared to be embarrassed by all the fuss made over them. Butch took the attention to himself and Claire as a good time to take control of the conversation regarding the overthrow of the local judge and his cohorts.

"Claire and I have asked the AG to assign an independent judge to sit as the authority in the upcoming trial of Judge Doran, the police chief, and the coroner. We must move fast so the suspects won't discover that they have been targeted for arrest. Our job is to round them up, hold them securely until they can get a fair trial of their peers, and administer justice." Butch and Claire were not accustomed to receiving that much attention for just doing their jobs, so they were both blushing a little. While Butch had thought that there might be hundreds of cult members hiding in the woods preparing to attack the people of Butler and Choctaw County at the whim of Judge Doran, he discovered that there were only a dozen or so full-fledged members who took orders directly from the judge. That made capturing and eliminating this cult easier than he had thought in the beginning. The trick was that they would have to arrest everyone at the same time, or there was a possibility that someone would messenger other members and there would be a bloodbath of bullets and bodies strewn in the streets of Butler.

"Here's the plan. We have assigned each of you a particular person to follow and apprehend at a specific time which I will tell you. Coordination is our very best tool to make this work perfectly." Claire handed each of the police officers and highway patrol personnel a picture of the person for whom they were going to arrest. "This will be a state operation, and thus a county judge cannot override these arrest warrants. In fact, there is an arrest warrant for Judge Doran as well. We would prefer that each person be taken alive, without gunfire, if possible. However, each of these people are considered armed and dangerous. If you pull your service weapon, I'd suggest you shoot to kill, because that's what they will be doing. Every one of you should have a Kevlar vest issued from either the highway patrol office or from Sheriff Phillips' office. That fact alone will not prevent you from being wounded or possibly killed if fighting breaks out, but these vests will prevent serious injury to body mass, your heart, major organs, and such. Are there any questions?" A voice called out from the rear of the room.

"Who gets to arrest the judge?"

"That will be Claire and my duty. I don't expect him to go down easily. From what I understand, he is a war veteran and has a small arsenal of weapons in his home. Just remember, always keep you cell phones and radios on and active. We anticipate making this move tomorrow morning around 10:00 AM, but I'll tell you when it's 'go time.' When you get that signal, move in quickly. We chose a time when most of these people will be out of their homes and at work. They will have less ability to fight back without their personal arsenals which they keep hidden at their homes. If there's nothing else, just be careful and be ready." Butch dismissed the officers, wishing them all the best results, and he and Claire decided to walk across the street to Lulu's Diner and get a cup of coffee. It was getting close to dinnertime, and Butch and Claire were looking forward to enjoying a nice Charlotte Phillips preparation, kicking off their shoes, and sipping sherry on the front porch before retiring to their bedroom. When they arrived at the B&B, they noticed a big difference from the last time they were there. When they had left in the morning, all the kids and Ruby had been sleeping, and the house was as quiet as always. However, when they got to The Jasmine House that afternoon, there seemed to be kids everywhere. They were running, playing, and making lots of noise. Ruby tried to quiet them down, but Claire just laughed and reassured her that she and Butch understood that kids must be kids.

"Don't worry about the noise for our sakes," Claire said. "It's good to hear laughter and giggling in these dark times. Did Leroy get here?" Ruby smiled and said yes. She thanked Claire and Butch for rescuing her family from the cult. Ruby said that Leroy had taken some medicine and had fallen asleep in their room. They had talked about the relocation by the U.S. Marshals, and they were ready to start their new life as soon as possible. Claire patted Ruby on the back and told her that would happen sooner than she might expect. Butch and Claire poured a glass of sherry and headed for the front porch. They would wait in the relatively quiet front porch area until dinner was served.

Chapter 16

The Raid

When people speak of a raid, they usually mean that a local night spot, a honky-tonk, or a bar has been set upon by the police to either break up a fight or dissolve an illegal clandestine operation. The problem with Sheriff Phillips' raid was that it was taking place all over the city of Butler and Choctaw County. Butch and Claire had spoken once more to Chief Laughing Bear, and the chief reassured them that none of his people had taken an active role in any of the extortion or other illegal activities the cult had been doing over the years. His people were simply co-sufferers of the government system which kept taking away their lands and their rights as Native Americans. Because they were considered 'colored' like the African American people, they could never belong to a White Supremacist cult. In other words, they were being used as potential sacrifices if someone ever came to dissolve their hidden cult. The white man would sacrifice them just as he had killed their forefathers, as they took over the rightfully owned land of the Native American Indians. Once explained to the chief by Butch and Claire, Chief Laughing Bear forbid any of his people from getting involved with the cult which was hiding out in the woods of Choctaw County. The chief went one step further in declaring that if they saw any of the cultists operating in the surrounding areas of Choctaw County, his tribe would capture them and bring them to the sheriff's office. This eliminated the ability of the cult members to run into the woods and hide from the authorities. They would be running into certain capture. Because of Leroy's help in identifying his co-conspirators, they were able to pinpoint every active cult member in the county. Now, they just had to isolate them and bring them to justice.

The morning was overcast and warm for a fall day, and Butch and Claire were not exactly sure how to dress for their activities. While they would not be tramping through the woods in search of cultists, they may have to run some of them down on the streets of Butler. Their main quest was to find, isolate, and arrest Judge Doran, hopefully, without incident. The more that they had discovered about the hidden cult in the woods of Choctaw County, the more they saw that the principal figure in the conspiracy was Judge Doran.

When they had been interrogating Leroy Smithson, he had explained to Butch and Claire how the hidden cult had been established, and why it was profitable to the judge. Leroy told them that the judge used blackmail and extortion to get businesses and individuals to do his bidding. He also had some of the trustees of the county jail work for him at his home for free and threatened them with longer jail sentences if they exposed the judge to public scrutiny. According to Leroy, the judge authorized the cult to poison Charles Phillips after one of the judge's bag men was tried and convicted of a crime which resulted in his incarceration at the prison in the Holman Correctional Facility in Atmore, Alabama. Hardened criminals made up the majority of the inmates at Holman, and the state of Alabama carried out the death penalty at the facility. It was the only facility in the state of Alabama authorized and equipped to execute male prisoners. Likewise, Tutwiler Prison in Russel County was the only authorized facility to put female prisoners to death. The female death row population comprised only three per-cent of all death row inmates in the state. When the man convicted of poisoning Charlotte Phillips husband was sent to Holman, the cult sent out a message throughout the county that there would be an eye-for-an-eye when it came to that man's death. The result was the murder of Charles Phillips. Leroy was prepared to testify to that statement when the trial of the cult members, to include Judge Doran, was held in the Choctaw County later that year. Right now, Butch and Claire needed to seize the judge before he could order any more damage to the county's residents who resisted his control.

Everyone in Alabama knew that the highest-ranking public figure in any county was the sitting county judge. In smaller counties, like Choctaw and others not included in major metropolitan areas of the state, the sitting county judge was the last word in justice and authority. If someone intended to remove such a powerful political person from his office and his control of the policing authority granted to him by the people of his county, it would take a state or federal mandate to do so. The last thing that Sheriff Phillips wanted was to have F.B.I. agents running around his county looking for wrongdoing. The state boys were easier to work with, and the governor had the authority to suspend any elected official until a review by the State Attorney General was completed and the official was either exonerated or proven guilty of the crimes he was being accused of doing. No special arrest warrant had to be issued, but acknowledgment by the state AG's office had to back up such an arrest to keep the judge in question incarcerated during the investigation. Butch and Claire had sought and received such authorization, and they expected to seize the judge while he was holding court in the Choctaw County Courthouse that morning.

Butch looked at his watch. It was 10:00 AM, and he texted the officers to begin their sweep of the cult members. He asked them to retain their quarry in their service vehicles until requested by the sheriff to bring them into the courthouse for their physical detention. At that same moment, Butch and Claire appeared in the main courtroom in the Choctaw County Courthouse, warrant in hand, to arrest and detain Judge Louis Doran. As they entered the courtroom, they noticed that the room was dark, and no lights had been turned on. Butch saw a deputy sheriff standing guard at the door of the courtroom, and Butch asked him why court was not in session.

"Your guess is as good as mine," he said. "The judge didn't show up, so all the cases on the docket for today were dismissed. There were some happy D.U.I. suspects and speeders as they left the courthouse. In this county, if at your court trial the police officer doesn't show up to testify, or if the judge is not in attendance, your potential violation of the law is excused for lack of evidence. We have no idea where Judge Doran is today, because he did not tell anyone that he was not coming in to work." Claire looked at Butch with concern as they thanked the officer and exited the judge's courtroom. Butch's cell phone rang, and he recognized the sheriff's number.

"Sheriff? What's up?" Butch spoke into the cell phone.

"We have good news and some bad news. The good news is that we have arrested most of the targeted men on our list of cult members. They are in custody in the vehicles of the officers who picked them up."

"That is good news! What's the bad news?"

"We think that Judge Doran has found out about the sting and may be planning to go into hiding so we can't find and arrest him."

"That's a coincidence you should say such a thing. Claire and I just visited his courtroom in the courthouse, and he didn't come in at all today. He left no instructions as to why he would be absent, and all the cases on his court docket today have been dismissed. How did you determine that he had gotten wind of the big sting operation? The only people who knew about it were our people—your officers and the AHP officers."

"We discovered a security leak in our office. We caught one of our junior officers placing a phone call to the judge, warning him about the sting which was happening today. As far as we can tell, he is in the wind."

"I don't think so, Sheriff," Butch said.

"What do you mean? Did you find him?"

"No, but he's not that kind of guy. He will make some last stand somewhere and try to go out in a blaze of glory. That's what he preached to his cult followers, and that's what he will do. It will be like Ruby Ridge if Judge Doran has any say in the way he is killed. I don't think he will surrender under any circumstances."

"Interesting thought, Butch. So, how do we smoke him out?"

"I don't think you will have to do anything for him to reappear. As soon as he thinks he has a foolproof plan, he will contact us."

"If you really think that is the case, then we need to begin to bring these felons into the county courthouse and have them arraigned. I got a text from the AG in Montgomery just a few minutes ago. They are sending down a judge to work on our behalf until we get all of this straightened out with Judge Doran. He is on his way now and should be in the Choctaw County Courthouse within the hour."

"Great! I'll put the word out for everyone to bring their detainees to the courthouse immediately. It will take a few hours to get everyone processed before they can be arraigned." Butch brought Claire up to date on the things that Sheriff Phillips had told him, and Butch sent everyone a text message to start bringing their prisoners back to the courthouse.

The cult members were brought to the courthouse in handcuffs and leg restraints. There were eleven in all, with one casualty of gunfire when he drew down on an Alabama Highway Patrolman. Unfortunately for the cultist, the AHP officer was the best shot in his unit, landing two well placed shots in the head and neck of his potential attacker. The other eleven criminals were fingerprinted, photographed, and booked on multiple offensives. The state charges would be heard in the Choctaw County Courthouse by visiting Judge Andy King, the AG's judge on loan from Montgomery. The federal charges, to include extortion, attempted murder, and murder in the first degree, would be heard by a federal court judge once the state of Alabama was finished with each of the cultists. It didn't matter how good their lawyers were because Judge King held each of the suspects without bond, remanding them to the county jail until their trials were held in Butler later that year. It took the remaining hours of the afternoon to get everyone fingerprinted and checked into the county jail, and by the time Butch and Claire left the courthouse for The Jasmine Inn, it was after 6:00 PM. Charlotte usually fed everyone dinner at 5:00 PM, but they were sure she would accommodate them for beginning the task of bringing her husband's murderer to justice. A very exhausted Claire Cavendish looked over at Butch and sighed.

"What was the dinner menu at The Jasmine House tonight? Do you remember what Charlotte said she was preparing? While I am very tired, I am also famished!"

"I agree with you on both counts. At first, I thought I was too tired to eat, but then I remembered how good Charlotte cooks, and I decided I have the strength to eat dinner, but I have no idea what's on the menu," he chuckled.

"By the way, Butch. When we ever get married, don't expect me to cook like Charlotte Phillips. It is physically impossible for a concert pianist to have such skills!" Claire leaned over and gave Butch a peck on the cheek.

"Claire, I have only known one other woman who could cook like Charlotte Phillips. She's been dead since 1987."

"Your mom?" He nodded nostalgically. "You still miss her after all these years?"

"I miss her a bunch, but what I really miss is her cooking. She was the best. If you can imagine someone who cooks better than Charlotte Phillips, then you can imagine my mother. She was the best!"

"You never talk about your upbringing. Tell me more about your family when you were growing up in Ashburn, Alabama."

"My dad was a welder, and he worked for the L&N Railroad for many years. It no longer exists now, having been acquired by the Seaboard Coast Line Railroad in the 1980s. He was a boilermaker."

"What the heck is a boilermaker? He made boilers for the railroad?" Butch laughed. He had explained this railroad term to many people over the years, and this would simply be one more time he took pride in telling how his father had kept the engines running for many years with his welding prowess.

"Until the late 1950s, railroad engines were mostly steam engines. They were eventually replaced by diesel locomotives by the 1960s, but steam engines were the principal energy generators for railroads, as well as seagoing vessels. The tanks on the steam engines were under extreme pressure, and when cracks would begin to appear on the outside of the tanks, my father would weld the cracks shut to keep the tanks working and creating the steam pressure needed to drive the wheels of the engines or the ships' turbines. He had a skill, but he had no formal education beyond the eighth grade. That's why he insisted that my brother and I go to college and improve our ability to get a better job and have a more secure financial success for our families."

"And your mom?"

"My mom was a totally different case. She never learned to drive an automobile, so she was totally dependent on her kids to drive her around when my father wasn't available to take her on her errands. She mastered one thing in life that no one else was able to do quite as well, and that was cook. She was the best cook I have ever known, and her food was a thing of legends. No one wanted to cook for her, because they could never come up to her standards of excellence. Charlotte Phillips gets close, but mom was still the best."

"See, I've known you for more than a year and you are just now telling me about your upbringing."

"It wasn't anything special. Just hardworking people trying to make their way through life as best they could. I was fortunate enough to have parents who taught me right from wrong, and that morality was important. They were better role models than I have become myself, but it's not because they didn't do their part well."

Butch and Claire finally arrived at The Jasmine Inn at 7:00 PM. They were afraid that they would be too late for Charlotte to serve them dinner, but things worked out well for them. The Smithson family had already eaten and had returned to their rooms for the evening, so the main part of the house was quieter than it had been the day before. Charlotte met them at the door with glasses of sherry, encouraged them to sit on the porch while she prepared their dinners, and gave them an overview of the menu for that night's dinner.

"You are having my homemade chicken and dumplings, fresh corn, green bean casserole, mashed potatoes and gravy, and your choice of beverage. I have just brewed a pot of tea, and you have a choice of blackberry cobbler or apple pie for dessert. How does that sound?"

"Marvelous, Charlotte," Claire said. Butch agreed, lifting his glass of sherry to her in a gesture of a salute.

"How did you day go? Were you able to catch some of those criminals who are stalking the innocent people of Butler and Choctaw County?"

"Even better than that, Charlotte," Butch said. "We have arrested most of the cultists who were hiding out in the woods in Choctaw County, and we have an arrest warrant for Judge Louis Doran. We simply must find him before we can begin to bring him to justice."

"Do you think he will surrender to you and your group?"

"Actually, no I don't," Butch said solemnly.

"Do you think he has fled the area and will try to evade capture? I understand he has a lot of money and can probably buy his way out of the county and the country if he has a notion to do so."

"As I told Sheriff Phillips, I don't think Judge Doran is the kind of man who runs from a fight. He is so deluded in his beliefs that he will try to set up a situation where he can go out in a blaze of glory, much like those radicals did at Ruby Ridge in Texas a few years ago. For now, he has decided to flee and hide himself while he puts a plan together. I expect him to reappear with some diabolical plan to get lots of attention before he commits suicide by cop."

"He's that unstable?"

"What do you think? You know these people much better than Claire and I ever will know them. We were able to arrest most of the suspected members of that cult without firing a shot. One of them tried to draw down on an Alabama Highway Patrolman, and he met his fate quickly. Unfortunately for the perp, he picked the best marksman in the local unit to try and face off in a handgun encounter. He was shot dead at the point of the attempted arrest. However, we have eleven others in custody, they have been fingerprinted and arrested, and they will all be arraigned in the Choctaw County Courthouse tomorrow morning in front of Judge Andy King."

"Who is Judge Andy King? I don't think I know him, and I know everyone in Butler," she asked.

"We had the Alabama AG send him to town to try these cultists and Judge Doran, assuming we can ever locate him and bring him to justice."

"What happens if you don't find Judge Doran?"

"Oh, he'll turn up sooner or later. His ego is too great for him to slink off into the dark and disappear from the public eye. No, I expect to hear from him soon!" Butch reassured her.

"Is there any way we can reopen the case on Charles' death? I still think if there were an autopsy on his remains that we would discover that he was poisoned by the judge and his minions."

"There are many things that must happen before we can attempt to exhume Charles' body for an autopsy, but I promise that I will do everything in my power to see that your wish is eventually granted by the new judge. He will have his plate full for the time being, but eventually, he'll probably issue a ruling to have Charles' body exhumed and examined for possible foul play."

"That would be great. I want to put this whole thing to rest eventually. I cannot get closure on Charles' death until that happens. Speaking of a full plate," Charlotte picked up on Butch's earlier comments, "your dinner will be ready in five minutes. Enjoy your sherry, wash your hands, and come to the table for your dinner."

Chapter 16

The Standoff

Dinner had been spectacular last night, with the wonderful smells and flavors of the old South. Southern cooking at its best, with fresh vegetables, hand rolled dumplings with chicken, and an unbelievable blackberry cobbler with vanilla ice cream. Butch hadn't remembered cobbler like that since he was a boy in Ashburn feasting at his parent's table on Sunday after church. While his mother was cooking all week, no other day of the week could compare to the Sunday dinner she served every week without fail. Roast beef, rice, gravy, fresh corn cut off the cobb, green beans from their freezer, fried chicken, mashed potatoes, and homemade dinner rolls which she started early in the morning, letting them rise in the window on sunny days, and finishing them off in her oven was the general fare every week. While Mike grew up somewhat poor, there was always more food to go around than anyone needed to consume. And while Charlotte's dinner last evening wasn't quite as complete as his mothers on any given Sunday, the comparison of quality was surely there. After their difficult day rounding up criminals, the heavy meal and quick shower they both took put them to sleep like a sleeping pill. Mike couldn't remember rolling over during the night, much less getting up to go to the bathroom. He was surprised that both would sleep so soundly with all the mayhem going on around them. Awakened by the sunlight streaming through the eastern window in their room, he intended to shake Claire to make sure they would not be late for breakfast, but her side of the bed was empty. Sitting up in the bed, Butch heard the water running and knew Claire had beat him into the bathroom to begin getting ready for the day's adventure.

While this diversion from their planned vacation was anything but restful, he felt like they had accomplished a lot breaking up the invisible cult which had plagued the city of Butler and Choctaw County for years. Working with Claire was so second nature to him that any day with her was like a vacation to some extent. He thought he might be falling in love with his business partner. He would keep those thoughts to himself for the time being. The door opened from the bathroom and steam came tumbling out like it was a steam bath. Claire had a towel wrapped around her hair, but otherwise she was butt naked.

"What a nice sight for these sore eyes," he said. "You are truly beautiful this morning." Claire gave him a wink and then dashed his hopes of anything amorous that morning.

"As much as I would like to climb back into bed with you and play house, we need to get going and have our breakfast before the entire Smithson family arrives at the breakfast table." Butch reluctantly agreed with her about beating the Smithson family to the food, but he also was tempted to grab Claire and pull her back into bed. He thought better of that idea, got up immediately, and shuffled into the bathroom to get ready for breakfast. In ten minutes, they were both dressed and ready to face the day. They slipped out of their room as quietly as possible, hoping to avoid running into the Smithson's.

"Good morning," they heard Charlotte say as they approached the breakfast table. "Did you two sleep well last evening?"

"Yes, and we are ready to take on whatever this day has in store for us," Claire said. "Have your other guests been down this morning?"

"The Smithson family?" Charlotte asked.

"That's the one," Butch laughed as he answered. "We were hoping to eat and get out of their way before they ascended upon your dining room."

"They are no longer here," Charlotte said. "They left at 6:00 AM this morning. I fed them at 5:00 AM, the U.S. Marshals came for them an hour later, and they disappeared into the early morning Choctaw County fog. I'm surprised that we didn't wake you with all the noise we were making getting them off on their journey. After he settled down, Leroy proved to be nice guy. I think all the pressure he was getting from that cult he was involved in made him crazy. He seemed like an ordinary guy this morning when they left with the U.S. Marshals."

"I'm sorry I didn't get to say goodbye to Ruby and the kids. They seemed to really appreciate the opportunity to leave Butler and Choctaw County. I'm assuming you have no idea where they went," Claire said.

"The entire family is in protective custody, and the marshals said that they would be relocated somewhere out west in a few days. Ruby and Leroy will have to reappear and testify in court about the cult when that case comes up, assuming the case goes to trial."

"I can't imagine why it wouldn't go to trial, can you?" Butch asked.

"According to Leroy, the guys in the cult are lost without their leader. If Judge Doran doesn't show back up, the members may all take a plea deal, and that would negate the need for Leroy or Ruby to come back and testify."

"I'm afraid we haven't heard the last of Judge Louis Doran," Claire said. "Like Butch has said, that judge is such a megalomaniac that he will reappear soon to try and take out his revenge on whoever he thinks caused the breakup of his little criminal domain. It's just a matter of when, not if, he will return."

"I hope you're wrong, but I don't doubt your expertise when it comes to cases like this one. That judge is not right in the head," Charlotte said.

"That's something we can all agree on, Charlotte," Butch said. "At this point, Claire and I are finished in our investigation of the invisible cult of Choctaw County, now that it has been exposed and dismantled by your local police department with help from the AHP. We will stay here for most of the morning and write up our report for both our boss in Ashburn and Sheriff Conrad Phillips. After that, we will head back to Ashburn to our jobs in the city."

"You never said what those jobs were, Mike," Charlotte said.

"I am the Chief of Police for the city of Ashburn, and Claire is my Chief of Detectives. We were on our way to Gulf Shores for a much-needed vacation when our boss, Mayor Sam Hannity of Ashburn, asked us to stop by and visit with your sheriff to see if we could be of assistance to him. The rest of the story you know by now."

"You gave up your vacations to come to Butler's aid?"

"Our boss and Sheriff Phillips have been friends for some time, and he reached out to our boss for help. We were on our way down Interstate 65 when our boss got the call. We had hoped to wrap up our involvement sooner, but we did what we promised our boss we would do, and now we need to go back home and resume our jobs with the city of Ashburn," Butch said.

"Are you going to get your vacation time back?" Charlotte asked.

"According to our boss, we will get to reschedule our trip to the beach as soon as we get the backlog of duties caught up in Ashburn. Hopefully, that will be soon, and we will be headed south again to the beach," Claire said.

"You know you are both welcome at The Jasmine Inn any time you're headed this way."

"Except for the rotten highways from I-65 to Butler, we would take you up on that offer," Butch said. "We have truly enjoyed our stay at The Jasmine Inn, and the food was fabulous! We are so spoiled on your cooking that we will miss it as much as everything else combined about Butler."

"You're too sweet," Charlotte said, blushing like a new bride.

Butch and Claire ate their breakfast in peace and quiet, not something that they had figured would happen this morning. Butch was not surprised that the U.S. Marshal serves whisked the Smithson family away in the early morning hours without warning. That's usually how they worked.

After breakfast, Butch and Claire went back to their room, began writing up their report, and sipping on another cup of coffee they had taken back to their room from the breakfast table, when a bulletin came rolling across the television set in their room. Claire noticed it first and alerted Butch. They watched the local television talking head explain about a standoff which was happening in Butler, Alabama. The camera feed was live, and the face of the captor was none other than Judge Louis Doran.

"Turn the volume up, Butch," Claire said. "It looks like your prediction is coming true." Judge Doran had set up a camera feed, was transmitting it to the local TV news outlet, and was stating why he was doing what he was doing.

"I am the rightful circuit judge of Choctaw County, and I have been dispatched by some outsiders who think that they are doing the people's will by trying to remove me from the bench. These are people who have come into our city of Butler, our sacred county of Choctaw, and who want to push the government's wishes upon us to allow unauthorized changes in our lifestyles which we have enjoyed for more than 150 years. First, they took the land of the Choctaw Indians in the 1800s and sent them packing to Oklahoma on the Trail of Tears. Then, after the War between the States, I refuse to call the war from 1861 to 1865 the Civil War, because there was nothing civil about the war or the failure of the government reparations afterward, the government sponsored Carpetbaggers to come into our land and steal from us. We decided to put a stop to those practices several years ago, and we went back to the laws as prescribed in the Holy Bible—'an eye for an eye, and a tooth for a tooth.' I have been duly elected by the people of Butler and Choctaw County several times because they believe in what we are doing to protect their God given rights." Doran kept spouting his manifest of beliefs, all the while standing in front of Pastor Ronald Smith, who was tied to a chair in front of the alter of the Butler Lutheran Church. It was obvious to everyone who had frequented that facility that Judge Doran had placed the pastor in a position at the alter as if he were to be sacrificed for some wrong which he had done to the people of Choctaw County. Doran had a sharp sickle-type of knife with a long-curved blade in his hand, and he had placed a bowl under the pastor's chair.

"What is he doing?" Claire asked in disbelief.

"It appears that he is going to sacrifice Pastor Smith for having given up information about the judge's invisible cult to us, therefore leading to the arrest of his members and his own removal from the county bench."

"On television? How does he think he can escape punishment for that if hundreds or thousands of people see him take the pastor's life?"

"You are thinking rationally, but Judge Doran is thinking like a demigod. He believes that he is an offspring of God and has the right and the duty to do God's will on Earth."

"Who in their right mind would ever believe him? Have you ever heard of such a thing in the past?"

"Sure. According to the dictionary, Achilles thought he was the son of Peleus, king of Myrmidons, and a sea nymph named Thetis. Remember the saying 'Achilles' heel?' According to legend, Achilles' mother held him by his heel and kept dipping him in the river Styx to make him immortal."

"And what is the Achilles' heel of Judge Doran?"

"Greed and pride. Those are also two of the seven deadly sins the Roman Catholic Church has been expounding for centuries. All seven of them are pride, greed, lust, envy, gluttony, wrath, and sloth, and I'm not sure the judge doesn't possess all of them, but his actions reveal his lust and envy for pride and greed."

"Who knew you were such a scholar?" Claire said. "And I thought you were just a flyboy with a desire to see the world and bomb the bad guys out of existence!" she said with a chuckle.

"I'm that, too," he smiled. "But I studied the classics, along with philosophy and theology when I was at Ashburn University. I made an A in all my philosophy classes."

"Of course, you did," Claire smiled. "Now, what are we to do with Judge Doran before he kills an innocent pastor for trying to do the right thing?"

"I'm not sure, but we can't do it here. Let's finish getting dressed and get over to the Butler Lutheran Church as quickly as possible." Butch saw Claire dress, make up her face, and was ready to walk out the door towards his pickup truck in ten minutes flat.

"How's that for getting ready in a hurry?" she asked Butch as she slid into the cab of his truck beside him.

"If I hadn't seen it myself, I wouldn't have believed it. Does this mean I can count on your getting ready like that in the future?"

"Not on your life, Butch. You know, a girl's got to keep her man waiting a while to make the anticipated meeting perfect," she cooed.

"Baloney," Butch said. "That's fine. At least I know if you absolutely, positively must get ready in less than thirty minutes, it can be done!" Claire just batted her eyes at him and acted as if she hadn't heard a thing he had said. She knew she wasn't fooling Butch, but it was fun trying. Claire looked at the speedometer and saw that Butch was driving twice the speed limit through town.

"Aren't you afraid that you will get pulled over for speeding?"

"Nah. I was hoping that some policeman would give me an escort through town, but since we are pulling up in front of the church, I guess we don't need an escort now." They both bounded out of the truck, but their way to the sanctuary of the Butler Lutheran Church was blocked by several local police cars, a few AHP officers, and the press.

"Hey, please let us through," Claire and Butch demanded as they showed their IDs and detective credentials to the surrounding hoard of watchers. "We are vital to this man's survival inside," Claire continued. Evidently, one of the officers in the crowd recognized them and officially guided them to the front of the mass of people who had gathered around the front of the church to see what was going to happen. Butch was not too fond of those who found others' problems a chance for entertainment, so he encouraged the police officers to break up the crowd, for the cameras to be turned off, and for he and Claire to be given the opportunity to talk Judge Doran down from the frenzy he had reached inside the church with Pastor Smith.

"Why should we stop filming? It's a free country!" one of the newscasters said while shoving a microphone into Butch's face.

"Unless you would like for that microphone to be inserted into an orifice of yours which is unaccustomed to such entries, I suggest you turn your camera off, cut the feed to the local television station, and let us try and save that man's life. What you and your fellow newscasters are doing is giving a megalomaniac a stage on which to operate. As long as you are here, Pastor Smith's life gets closer and closer to a tragic end. If the judge discovers that no one is hearing his ranting and threats, he may relent and let the pastor go. Otherwise, the pastor is definitely doomed, and that will be on your hands and your network's hands. Do you understand me?"

"You're asking me to ignore the story of the year in Butler, Alabama? And why would I do that?"

"Because if anything happens to that man in there being held hostage, I will personally make it my life's goal to paste you with it for the remainder of your career. Now, do I make myself clear?" The reporter dropped his microphone, backed away from the front of the church, and told his people to shut down the transmission. When Butch saw what the reporter had done, he thanked him and gave him a thumbs-up signal.

"What do you suggest that we do now, Butch?" Sheriff Conrad Phillips was asking. The sheriff had shown up during the altercation between the reporter and Butch, so this was the first time the two of them had spoken about the hostage crisis.

"Sheriff, there are two things that may happen inside no matter what we do out here. The judge may kill Pastor Smith no matter what we do, or we may distract him long enough for someone to target him with a long-range rifle shot. Do you have a marksman among your troops?"

"I do. What's your plan?"

"If we try to storm the church, I believe that Judge Doran will kill the pastor immediately. However, right now he thinks his kidnapping and threats to Pastor Smith are being viewed by hundreds and thousands of people. If he discovers that that is not the case, we may have a chance to change the scenario from him controlling the events to our controlling them."

"I'm listening."

"See that building over across the street?" Butch pointed to a three-story brick building facing the Butler Lutheran Church.

"Yeah. I see it."

"Let's put your sharpshooter in one of those windows. We will entice the judge to bring Pastor Smith to the front door so we can see that he is still alive. Once we get him there, you man will have a chance of taking him out."

"What if he misses?"

"Then the pastor dies, one way or the other. Either your man accidentally hits him, or the judge survives and kills the pastor and himself. It's not a great option, but I can't think of another one, can you?" The sheriff shook his head no.

"First, I have to set things up so Judge Doran will see the need to come to the front of the church, and I will need a bullhorn for that." The sheriff had one of his deputies produce a bullhorn for Butch to speak through, and he watched as the drama began to unfold. "Make sure your man is ready before I begin speaking to the judge." The sheriff looked across the street and saw that his sharpshooter was there, tucked into a concealed area behind one of the open windows on the third floor.

"We're as ready as we're ever going to be Butch," the sheriff said. "Let's get this started." Butch nodded, winked at Claire, and put the bullhorn close to his lips.

"Judge Doran. This is Detective Butch Todd, special agent representing the state of Alabama and the governor's office. Can you hear me?" There was silence for a moment and then a voice rang out.

"Yes, I hear you. What do you want? You know I'm going to kill this man who betrayed our cause, and everyone in Choctaw County, as well as many more throughout the world, will see justice served!"

"That's not going to happen, Judge."

"You don't think I have the nerve to kill this man?" he roared.

"Yes, I think you can kill him, but no one is going to see it. The computer feed from your camera to the television stations has been interrupted and will not be reconnected, no matter what you do in there. If you're going to make a statement like killing a man, you should do it with an audience. Don't you agree?"

"What do you mean?"

"Well, unfortunately, there is a crowd outside the church who wants to see bloodshed, and unless you bring your hostage to the door and kill him there no one is going to see anything."

"You're bluffing!"

"No sir. I don't bluff. If there is a television in your building, you can check it out. You have had all of the free publicity that you will ever get, so you might as well either let your hostage go free, or you can bring him out to the front of the building and sacrifice him there. The way I see it, those are your only two choices." Nothing seemed to happen for a few moments, and then the front door of the sanctuary began to open slowly. The pastor was the first person anyone could see, and then Judge Doran could be seen behind him with a sharp knife, wielding it around as if the judge were a butcher.

"In accordance with the rights afforded every man in the Holy Scriptures, I will now sacrifice this man for his wrongdoings against the people of Choctaw County and the city of Butler." As the judge began to move the blade towards the neck of the pastor, one shot rang out which quieted the large crowd. A small red circle began to appear just above the judge's eyes, and he crumpled down behind the pastor. Pastor Smith ran for his life to safety, hiding himself among the people in the crowd. As anticipated, the news crew began to run towards the church and try to push their way into the nave to observe the horrible site of the most powerful judge in Choctaw County with his brains blown all over the entrance to the nave. Butch and Claire blocked the door, backed up by the sheriff and his men.

"No one is going inside the church for the moment," Butch said. "It is a crime scene, and it is also a sacred space that doesn't need the likes of you people tramping around inside of it. Sheriff Phillips will have a statement for you from the Choctaw County Courthouse steps within the hour. Please don't make a nuisance of yourself, because after the week we've had, we really would hate locking you up in the jail until the new judge can arraign you for disorderly conduct and obstruction of justice." There were rumblings among the crowd, but everyone did as Butch had instructed them. Sheriff Phillips looked over at Butch and gave him a thumbs up signal.

"Sheriff, why don't you make your way over to your office, comprise whatever statement you wish to give to the press and all these gawkers, and Butch and I will work with the coroner until we get this matter cleared up? How does that sound to you?"

"Great. I don't think we would have ever cracked this case if you and Butch had not stopped by on your way to Gulf Shores for your vacation. I'm going to put in a good word for both of you with Sam Hannity and tell him he needs to restore your vacation time, and give you a bonus for being so helpful," Conrad said.

"Just getting the vacation time back will be enough. We're glad that we could be of assistance," Butch said.

The sheriff headed off towards his office, and Butch and Claire went inside to survey the damage from the sharpshooter's bullet. They had one of Sheriff Phillips' men guard the door, and they also requested that the entire parking lot and church be taped off with yellow crime tape to discourage nosy neighbors from tampering with the crime scene. The coroner came, pronounced the judge dead at 2:35 PM, and Butch and Claire left him with the corpse. Butch looked down at his watch and realized that they had been negotiating with a crazy judge for more than four hours before the judge decided to commit suicide by cop.

"I guess our work here is done, Partner," Butch said to Claire.

"And I'm so glad it is. While I'd like to go on to the beach from here, I think we should reschedule with the mayor and get caught up on what we've missed with our own jobs in Ashburn for the past week."

"As much as I want to disagree with you, I'm afraid I can't. Let's have one last great Charlotte Phillips' dinner, get a good night's rest, and head back to Ashburn in the morning. I'll text the mayor and clue him in on what our plans are. I'm sure he'll be glad we're back on the job." Claire agreed, they got into Butch's truck, and they headed for The Jasmine Inn one more time.

Epilogue

Butch and Claire made it home in time to discover that all of their work had simply piled up while they were gone. They didn't really expect anyone else to cover for them, so they weren't really disappointed. After setting off for a pleasure trip to a romantic spot at Gulf Shores, winding up in a small and seemingly insignificant town to help their boss's friend, was quite an adjustment. Looking back, they were happy that they had been instrumental in helping restore Sheriff Conrad Phillips to his rightful and respectable place of authority, and no one was going to miss a corrupt and crooked circuit judge who simply went bad somewhere along his journey through life.

The feedback from the Choctaw County Courthouse was that newly installed Judge Andy King was fitting in quite well with the people of Butler and Choctaw County. There was a rumor that he might consider staying and running for a permanent job as Choctaw County Circuit Judge when the elections were held again in November. No one claimed the body of Judge Doran, and he was buried in the local cemetery with no fanfare and no headstone. No one wanted to remember anything about the judge's last few years on the bench. He had been terrorizing the county and Butler for many years, and it finally cost him his life.

Most of the cultists who had been captured and arrested were convicted of minor crimes, forced to serve time either in community service, or restricted with ankle monitors where they could only go to and from work and home without special authorization by the judge. "*When you cut off the head of the snake, the snake usually dies.*" Butch had heard that saying all his life, but now he finally understood what it really meant. There was no zeal left in Choctaw County to get instant justice for right and wrong.

The courts had become important again in the justice of the citizens of Butler and Choctaw County.

There was a comprehensive investigation of all county workers who had been either directly or indirectly supervised by Judge Louis Doran. With few exceptions, they had been extorted or threatened into cooperating with the judge. One good example was the coroner, who once refused to perform an autopsy on Charles Phillips at the request of his wife. He was now very willing to exhume and autopsy the remains of Charlotte's late husband, and the results were predictable. Charles had been poisoned with arsenic, and it would have been evident right after his death had the autopsy been allowed by the judge. Charlotte had filed a claim against Judge Doran's significant estate, along with many other citizens of Choctaw County. Fortunately, the judge had no living heirs Choctaw County, so there was a good chance that Charlotte would profit from all her grief and pain at the hands of such a tyrant. The only thing she had really wanted was justice for Charles.

Summer had turned into fall, and it was beginning to get cooler at night, and not so warm during the daylight hours. Butch and Claire were getting settled back into their jobs when Butch received a phone call from Major Bennington at the 117th Air Wing Command. He requested that Butch meet him the next day at The Crab Barrack for lunch. A new world was about to open up for Butch and Claire.

Made in the USA
Columbia, SC
09 March 2022